A FIND FOR ALL TIME

A FIND FOR ALL TIME

•

MARDI PARRISH

AVALON BOOKS
THOMAS BOUREGY AND COMPANY, INC.
401 LAFAYETTE STREET
NEW YORK, NEW YORK 10003

PRINTED IN THE UNITED STATES OF AMERICA
ON ACID-FREE PAPER
BY HADDON CRAFTSMEN, SCRANTON, PENNSYLVANIA

A FIND FOR ALL TIME

Chapter One

"I am not running away, Mother." Elizabeth jammed another stack of clothing into the suitcase that lay open on her bed. Two more tweed bags sat by her door.

"You're being absurd, Elizabeth." Victoria Way continued her litany of objections, still seated regally on the Chippendale chair by the fireplace in her daughter's bedroom. At forty-three, she was every bit as attractive and vivacious as her twenty-four-year-old daughter. "With only six months left until the wedding, there must be thousands of things to do. Such a wonderful boy," she sighed. "And from such a good family. This will be a marriage made in heaven—"

"It's a marriage made on Wall Street, Mother." Elizabeth's tone rang flat.

"And you should thank your guardian angel for Trevor," her mother's voice rose. He loves you. He is so right for you—"

1

"I know he is, Mother. He's a successful man, just like Daddy. He'll provide a beautiful home for me, and a secure future, make all my decisions for me, make all my new friends for me. What more could I ask for?"

Elizabeth tossed her lustrous chestnut hair over her slim shoulders. Picking up a tortoiseshell headband from her bed, she strolled to the wide bay window and gazed out at the green patch of New York's Central Park, stretched out far below.

The traffic on Fifth Avenue looked like a line of scurrying ants from her family's penthouse. She eyed the scene remotely while sliding the headband on, pulling her slightly longer than shoulder-length hair back. Its blunt trim lent an air of simplicity and sophistication that Elizabeth took for granted. A perfectly made-up, oval face reflected back at her from the window, its troubled expression unnoticed.

When she started seeing Trevor Davis, her parents were thrilled. Her father's investment company had done a small amount of business with Davis Brokers Limited, and he was very impressed with the size of the company Trevor would control one day. A cooperative relationship between the two companies would be beneficial to both, and the two families were well aware of this.

Trevor loved her, she knew that. It was just . . . overwhelming sometimes.

"I have to do this, Mother." Elizabeth spoke to her own reflection in the glass.

"Do what, Elizabeth?" The older woman's tone was becoming more acidic with each word. "Shirk your duties? Run off to some wretched, uncivilized place?"

"Uncivilized?" Sparks of rebellion flashed in Elizabeth's hazel eyes as she whirled around. "It's in Texas, for goodness sake. Just outside of a big city." Turning back to the window she continued, "This is my last chance to do something for my own selfish reasons, something I feel is important."

"And you feel digging around in the dirt for old bones is important enough to risk your entire future for? To risk your future with Trevor?"

"I'm not risking anything, Mother." Elizabeth leveled her tone again as she returned to her packing. "Trevor loves me. My working in Texas for the summer doesn't threaten my relationship with him at all."

"But even if that were true, you'll be spending the summer digging in dirt. Honestly, Elizabeth, it's no occupation for a lady."

"Archaeology is a perfectly respectable occupation, and one that I feel is important. Besides, I won't be doing much of the actual digging," she admitted with regret. "My job will be to assist Dr. Sutherland with his paperwork. I'll be cataloguing his finds and transcribing notes for the book he's working on. Much of the same things I do at the American Museum of Natural History."

The large window with its view of Central Park drew Elizabeth's gaze again. To the west, across the swath of green, hidden by dense foliage and distant haze, was the museum where Elizabeth worked as a volunteer every moment of her spare time. It was there that she could truly find peace and contentment. From the dioramas of the biology of man in the Margaret Mead Hall to the Star of India sapphire in the Hall of Minerals and Gems, Elizabeth never tired of working among the largest collection of artifacts in the world.

In Texas she would be helping to contribute to the store of information available to researchers, scholars and educators. The very idea filled her with a secret thrill. The whole experience of being in Texas would be so good for her. She intended to use her free time to explore the countryside of the west, to experience a lifestyle so very different from her own.

"But that's volunteer work, dear," Victoria explained slowly, as if speaking to a child. "It's quite something different to do it for pay."

"I realize you're unhappy about this, Mother, but I've made my decision. Are you coming with me to the airport? Daddy and Trevor have meetings tomorrow morning—as usual—and can't make it. I don't want to be seen off by the chauffeur."

"Elizabeth!" Victoria clutched a monogrammed handkerchief to her watering eyes.

"Oh, Mother, please understand." Elizabeth rushed over and knelt at her side. "I'm going tomorrow, and I need you to try to understand." She lay her head on the inconsolable woman's lap and felt the tender strokes of her mother's hand on her hair.

"I wish you would reconsider, Elizabeth. I wish I could see why you want to do this. Maybe then I could talk some sense into you."

The jeep hit another dip in the dry Texas riverbed and shot up into the air. All four wheels left the ground for a brief moment before slamming back to earth again. Ar-

chaeologist Burk Sutherland gripped the wheel tighter with
his broad hands and inched the accelerator lower.

"In a hurry, Burk?" Ned struggled to hold on to the
camera bag that bounced in his lap as his friend gunned
the jeep around a sharp bend, sliding on the sand. "You
know, I'd like to make it back to the dig in one piece."

Burk slowed the vehicle briefly as he glanced across at
his fellow archaeologist. They were both similar in appearance, but Burk topped his friend by two inches at six
feet even. But unlike Ned's affable, fair looks, Burk's dark
hair and smoky gray eyes gave him a somber, brooding
look that made him appear older than his thirty-two years.

"Sorry," he grunted, tight-lipped. "I've got my mind on
other things, I guess."

"Like your deadline?"

"I suppose," Burk steered the jeep out of the riverbed,
onto the narrow road they had left earlier that morning. The
brilliant red sandstone cliffs and deep green juniper bushes
of the Caprock region retreated behind them, replaced now
with the open, rolling plains. "The pictures we got today
of the Caprock formation put me close to finishing that
chapter of my book. I just need to polish up the text a bit."

"It's too bad Jean-Paul had to go back to France before
he could help you finish the book. But your new assistant'll
be here soon. He'll help you get things going again."

"My new assistant isn't a he," Burk replied, glaring into
the blazing Texas sunset. Bands of blue and gold stretched
upward from the red ball, like the eyelashes of a giant.

"But you told me—"

"I know what I told you," he snapped. Then allowed

his regret to soften his tone. "I'm not getting the assistant I requested from the director at the Archaeology Institute."

"Does the one they're sending you have good qualifications?" Ned asked in alarm.

"None that I could see on her resume. A ritzy Manhattan address, a finishing school in Europe, and absolutely no work experience."

"What're you going to do, Burk?"

"Make the most of it," he grimaced.

Standing outside in the central compound of the Lubbock Lake Site, Elizabeth tugged absently at her khaki shorts and straightened the collar of her cotton blouse. She glanced nervously around for any sign of Dr. Sutherland. Of course, she was fully aware that she had no idea what he looked like. On her arrival last night, she found a note from him taped to her door, commanding her to meet him here promptly at 7:00 A.M.

After the energetic tour of the facility with her new roommate, Clare, it was hard to drag herself out of bed before dawn this morning. But, somehow, she had arrived with plenty of time to spare.

Now she stood in the clearing surveying the cinder-block buildings that served as dorms for the archaeologists and students. Nearby was the low, brown building that housed office space for the research conducted here. Archaeologists and anthropologists came from all over the world to this small lake—the same one visited by animals and people for thousands of years.

"You made it," a deep voice with an edge of cynicism echoed across the deserted clearing. Elizabeth flinched in surprise and turned, searching for the speaker. A man, tall and earnest, stepped from the shadows of a cluster of elms.

Shielding her eyes against the morning sun, Elizabeth took a tentative step toward him. ''Dr. Sutherland?''

His eyes, a smoldering shade of gray, roamed over her face, as if he were committing every facet of her appearance to memory. Steeling herself against his intense inspection, Elizabeth stepped closer and offered him her hand. For a moment she saw disapproval flash across his aloof features, as if he would refuse to shake hands with her.

''Burk Sutherland,'' he said as he finally took her hand.

Cool skin caressed her, a surprising coolness that drew her senses out toward him. She tilted her head back and gazed up into the stern mask of his features, mesmerized by his commanding presence. A thatch of dark, unruly hair complemented his gray eyes, and hung over the rumpled collar of his work shirt. The moment his right hand freed hers, he raked strong fingers through the sides of his tangled mane. But it was no straighter when he finished.

''Elizabeth Way. I'm—''

''We'll be at the dig this morning.'' He turned his back on her and threaded his way among the trees. A canvas bag that hung casually over one shoulder bumped against his hip as he moved swiftly through the greenery. ''I have about three hours of work to do there, then we'll be spending the rest of the day in my office back here at the compound. You can type, I suppose?''

His long legs stretched out in a ground-eating stride as he lined out the itinerary for the day. Elizabeth tried to stretch her stride, without actually jogging, to get abreast of him. Still, she was a few steps behind him all the way.

Keeping her eyes trained on his boots, she watched them strike the ground with more force than seemed necessary, as if their owner needed to feel the impact he made on the earth with each step. His long, muscular legs pumped like iron pistons in their covering of faded denim jeans. No other fabric would have been durable enough to withstand the punishing pace he used, Elizabeth supposed.

She grinned at the silly notion that distracted her from Dr. Sutherland's orientation lecture. It was time to get her mind back on what she was here to do: work. A solid wall rose up in front of her just as she began berating herself for daydreaming, and she smacked right into it.

Stumbling back a step, Elizabeth managed to regain her balance in time to realize the solid wall she had hit was Dr. Sutherland's broad chest. He glared down at her, his balled hands resting on his narrow hips.

Heat flooded her cheeks, driving out the refreshing coolness that had inhabited her body ever since the elm clearing. Gathering every shred of dignity she had, Elizabeth squared her shoulders and stepped around him, continuing alone down the worn path they had been traveling at such a breakneck speed.

A few paces later she heard him following her, and he was soon very close behind, his silent presence unnerving her. ''You were saying?'' she prompted him.

''We'll be putting in long hours every day, and I need to make sure you understand that right now. If you feel this is more than you bargained for, or more work than you're prepared to do, I'd understand if you changed your mind about wanting to work here for the summer.''

What? He sounded as if he didn't want her here, almost as if he felt that she wouldn't be equal to the task. Distracted, Elizabeth caught her foot on a protruding root and nearly stumbled to her knees.

A sinewy arm shot out and caught her before she managed to regain her balance. She felt strong fingers curl about her upper arm, almost completely encircling it. Her gaze flew up to his chiseled features, and he released his grip instantly, stepping back from her at the same time.

''Are you all right?'' he asked, concern clearly visible on his face.

Or could it be guilt? A moment before, he seemed to be suggesting she give up her job and go home before she even got started. Irritation sent a flush to her cheeks.

''Yes,'' she calmly replied. ''I'm fine, Dr. Sutherland. Shall we continue?'' She turned her back on him and again struck out ahead on the trail, taking extra precautions when roots appeared in the path.

''Just so you understand what I'll be requiring of you, Miss Way.'' His tone had regained its sternness. ''Long hours, with a great deal of tedious work. You'll need to keep yourself available to me at all times, even late at night. I'll expect you with me at the dig sight to take notes early each morning. You'll be responsible for organizing and typing up the day's notes and having them ready for my review each evening.'' He paused as his stride matched hers.

''There'll also be several pages of my manuscript that I expect you to type every day. They must, of course, be letter-perfect. No white-out or erasures, you understand. This book I'm working on is very important to me, and I won't let anything stand in my way. I have to finish it in less than three months.''

The man sounded insufferable! Elizabeth worked at keeping her temper under control as they continued their tense march through the grove of elms surrounding the Lake Site. He was outlining enough tasks for an army of secretaries. And as far as ''keeping herself available to him at all times,'' she clenched her fists in frustration, that sounded perfectly ridiculous.

Maybe she should just quit. Just turn around and tell him right to his smug face that he should contact the Institute for another assistant this very minute. It would serve him right if it took the Institute a full three months to find someone and send them out here.

''Hello,'' a man called as he approached along the path. ''Burk.'' He waved, smiling openly as he drew nearer.

''Ned,'' Dr. Sutherland returned the other man's friendly greeting with a genuine smile. ''Everything all right down at the dig this morning?''

''Sure,'' the fair-haired man replied as his attention focused on Elizabeth. ''Ned Wilson.'' He engulfed her hand in his.

''Nice to meet you, Ned. I'm Elizabeth, Dr. Sutherland's new assistant.''

''For the day, at least,'' Burk added quickly, his smile dissolving into the stern look he had worn since she first met him in the compound.

Smiling with all the friendliness she didn't feel, Elizabeth faced him fully. ''For the summer,'' she corrected him sweetly. ''The entire summer.''

A stony, indifferent look replaced his stern mask as he absorbed Elizabeth's meaning.

Silently, she hoped this meant he chose to accept her presence here as his assistant. There really was no other choice for her, she knew. She couldn't bear the thought of packing up and returning to New York yet. This summer here in Texas, so far from the pressure she felt from her family and Trevor, meant too much to her. It had been all she thought about since making the spur-of-the-moment decision to apply for the job.

At one of the many receptions she attended at the museum, Elizabeth had stood listening to Wally Byrn, from the Archaeological Institute, discussing grant distributions. It all seemed rather boring until he mentioned that he also provided assistants to archaeologists who worked at various digs around the world. At that time he was looking for a replacement assistant for an archaeologist in Texas. The young man who had the job was called back to his home in France unexpectedly, due to family obligations.

Without giving herself time to consider the consequences, Elizabeth immediately asked Wally for a chance at the job. Less than two weeks later she was in Texas, standing on a dirt path beside her new boss, Dr. Burk Sutherland. It wasn't turning out as she had hoped it would, but she felt determined to make the best of the situation she had jumped into so blindly.

Dr. Sutherland scrutinized her speculatively for a moment, but Elizabeth refused to flinch from his smoky eyes.

She held her chin up and braced herself for the next round of arguments against her continuing as his assistant.

"For the whole summer?" He arched a doubtful brow at her.

"That's what I said," she replied calmly.

He rocked back on his heels for a moment, and crossed his muscular arms across his broad chest.

She couldn't prevent her eyes from wandering down to the corded muscles rippling under Dr. Sutherland's cotton shirt. His chest had been so hard when she bumped into it. . . .

"Then I'd suggest we get started, Miss Way. We have a lot to do and precious little time to do it in." Swinging by her, Burk gave his friend a curt nod before striking out down the path, quickly settling into his long, ground-covering strides.

Confusion filled her as she stared, open-mouthed at his retreating back. Could it really be that easy? Had he accepted her that readily?

"Don't let Burk get to you, Elizabeth." Ned smiled at her obvious bewilderment. "He's a man with a lot on his mind."

She glanced back at Ned's friendly face. "And he's a man in a hurry."

He instantly broke into peals of laughter and Elizabeth joined in. Ned gave her a real sense of rapport that instantly drove out her growing feeling of loneliness.

"Oh, Ned, thanks. I needed that." She turned back to the trail and suddenly realized Dr. Sutherland was out of sight.

"I'll see you later!" She threw the words over her shoulder as she set out in a fast jog after her new boss.

The dig wasn't much to look at to the untrained eye, Elizabeth noted. It was not far from the water's edge, in a small clearing, surrounded by low shrubs and towering elms. Four people were already at work in various sections of the dig. Part of the area was marked out in a grid pattern of meter-square units. Strings that stretched from pegs in the earth served as the boundary markers for the units.

But inside each unit, Elizabeth knew, excavators were uncovering objects of importance. Dr. Sutherland was on his knees near one of the units, removing a trowel and brush from his canvas bag. He would begin to carefully remove the sediment surrounding objects, layer by layer. The soil he removed would be bagged and taken to the compound to a special building where it would be washed through screens, to remove even the tiniest objects for his inspection.

Burk glanced up and managed to keep a look of annoyance off his face when he realized Elizabeth had followed him to the dig. She could have made his life a lot easier by going back to the compound with Ned.

His brush rolled out of his hand and he leaned over to retrieve it. Elizabeth snatched it up and held it out to him.

"Thanks," he snapped. So, now he knew one thing she would be good for. Too bad this job consisted of more than dropping things all the time.

It was also too bad he so desperately needed the grant money from the Archaeological Institute to finish his book. What pleasure it would give him to tell Elizabeth to go pack her designer bags with her designer clothes and get herself back to wherever she had come from. Then he could get on with his job.

What he needed was an assistant who wasn't afraid to
work. Someone like Jean-Paul who needed the work just
as much as he did, and was willing to do what it would
take to get the job done.

He had so much left to do. Scowl lines deepened across
his forehead. They had sprung into existence weeks ago
and stubbornly refused to leave his face. Burk absently
rubbed the bridge of his nose. It was still very early in the
morning and he already felt wound tight as a spring.

Pulling his clipboard from the tan canvas bag, Burk began checking his field drawing of the unit he knelt beside.

"Is this your normal morning routine?" Elizabeth boldly
stepped forward and peered over his shoulder.

Sighing with impatience, Burk lowered his clipboard and
tried not to glare too hard at her. To his surprise, she stared
coolly back at him. This wasn't going to be easy. It had
been so simple yesterday to declare to Ned that he would
make the best of this situation.

"It is, since my assistant went back to France." He
turned back to the drawing in his lap.

"Yes, I heard from Wally about you losing your assistant. He said you were concerned about falling behind on
your schedule."

So, Wally was the boyfriend at the Archaeological Institute. Burk felt his blood pressure climbing. Wally had
given this job to his little girlfriend as a nice summer vacation, and with pay. How convenient for Wally and Elizabeth.

Seething, Burk realized there was nothing he could do
about it now. He didn't have the money to hire a qualified
assistant himself. He was on a shoestring budget until this

book got finished. Every dime he had came through grants from the Institute. Somehow, he would have to get the job done with no help. He would have to, there was no other choice.

"Poor Wally was in a bit of a dither the day he processed my paperwork," Elizabeth continued.

Burk remained silent, determined to make it a one-sided conversation. Maybe if she got no response, she would quit rattling on and let him get back to work.

"He was so nervous. I had to take the papers home and finish them myself," she chuckled softly.

So Wally had been nervous. Burk glowered as he rummaged through his bag for a pencil as he absorbed Elizabeth's statement. Her "poor Wally" had probably been eaten up with guilt. He had given away a job that should have gone to someone qualified for it, someone who could work for a living.

Glancing at Elizabeth's immaculately manicured nails, Burk scoffed. Those weren't the hands of a person used to digging in the ground, used to getting dirty. Her lustrous chestnut hair was swept neatly back from her smiling face and held in place by a beige headband. He found it impossible to imagine her with mussed hair and smudged cheeks.

"It was a real shocker when his daughter delivered twins."

"His daughter?" Had he missed something? Burk suddenly realized that he should have been listening closer.

"Yes." Elizabeth eyed him curiously. "Wally's daughter went into labor while he was processing my papers. He wanted to get them done before going to the hospital to wait for her to deliver. Mother was in a state, too." Elizabeth smiled at the memory. "She and Wally's wife were classmates at Dartmouth, you see."

"No." He tried to sound polite. "I'm afraid you've lost me."

"Mother doesn't like to hear about any of her friends becoming grandparents."

"Oh." Burk turned his attention to his papers. Wally wasn't her boyfriend. He hadn't given the job to Elizabeth because he was trying to score points with his girlfriend. A stab of guilt worked its way deep into his gut. Moments earlier he had been thinking about Wally's guilt, and been almost gloating over the thought of the other man's discomfort. Well, now it was his turn to feel guilty.

But that bit of news didn't change one fact, he realized. Wally had given the job to someone who wasn't in the least bit qualified for it. Instead of a girlfriend, he had given it to a family friend, which was just as damning in Burk's eyes. Especially considering that Burk was the one who would ultimately pay for Wally's unfair actions. If he didn't reach the deadline, his career would suffer a major setback. Maybe he had given up too easily back on the trail. Should he try again to talk Elizabeth into quitting?

Burk felt a tingling sensation on his arm and reached down to swat away whatever insect had caused it, but his fingers stopped inches from their target. Elizabeth was leaning over his arm, intently studying the diagram he held. It was her lustrous hair that brushed delicately over his exposed flesh, sending sparks of tension through him. Sparks that burned as brightly as the ones he saw dancing in her hair.

Chapter Two

"Jean-Paul never had any trouble deciphering my handwriting." Dr. Sutherland rose from his imposing, cluttered desk and stalked over to the metal typing table Elizabeth sat hunched over. "He transcribed my notes with no complaints, and managed to stay up with each day's accumulation."

"But Jean-Paul isn't here." She managed not to grit her teeth as the words left her pursed lips. "And I probably wouldn't have any trouble either, if I could see over here in this dark corner."

A scowl stretched across his ruggedly handsome features as he glared down at the pages of scrawled notes. Elizabeth had been hard at work on them since he led her back here to his small office from the dig. "I can't see what the problem is," he huffed. His large form hulked over her as he squinted at the stack of papers piled by the typewriter.

"The problem is, I can't see," she glared up at him.

"The light bulb in this lamp can't be more than forty watts, and that's obviously not strong enough for this kind of work. It wouldn't be such a problem if this table were closer to the window, or even out under the ceiling light." Placing the table anywhere other than right where it sat would be impossibly inconvenient in this room. The whole space couldn't be larger than twelve feet square, she estimated.

Burk tapped the lamp over the small table and tried to tilt it to better illuminate the papers. "Jean-Paul never complained about it."

"I think we've already covered the fact that I'm not Jean-Paul." She reached up to the lamp and gave it a vigorous tug when he gave up.

"Yes, Miss Way, I can see that."

There was an odd hesitancy in his voice that caused her to glance up into his handsome face. His smoke-gray eyes drifted down to her throat, and became caught on the pulsing hollow just above the opening of her blouse. If they drifted any lower . . . She shifted away from him, covering her nervous actions by rearranging the cup of pens and pencils on the table.

He didn't move away. She could feel his moist breath on the back of her neck, and hear his lungs pumping in and out, like a blacksmith's bellows. Like his walking, it seemed to her that Burk Sutherland did everything as hard as he could. The air trembled around him with each breath, just as the earth vibrated with the concussion of his steps. He was a big man, and he made a big impact on everything surrounding him. He was unquestionably making a big impact on her, Elizabeth realized.

"You certainly don't smell like Jean-Paul." His voice rumbled, a low and sensual tone across the tingling lobe of her ear. "You smell like fresh nectarines."

His words, spoken so softly, almost slipped by her. She wasn't sure she heard them correctly at first. "It . . . it's my shampoo." With tiny movements, she plucked at the collar of her blouse. He inhaled deeply and Elizabeth froze, stunned at the confusing flush of feelings that were running through her.

The wooden bookshelf behind the table creaked as he leaned back against it for a moment. Roughly, he cleared his throat. "I'll go over to the supply room. There's probably a brighter bulb in there somewhere."

"No! Don't go," she blurted and sprang from her chair as he lurched to a stop in the doorway. Seeing the startled look on his face, she hastened to explain her outburst. "I'll go. I'm the assistant, and I should be doing the errands, not you." She realized her voice sounded brittle and frayed. What was she doing, ordering him to stay like that? He looked just as embarrassed as she felt right now.

After spending the morning trying to convince him that she was right for this job, Elizabeth felt completely unprepared to cope with being shut in an office with the man who was setting her nerves on edge. Keeping her eyes averted from his compelling face, she managed to squeeze between him and the doorway without quite touching his broad frame.

She felt his eyes burning into her back as she stepped out into the sunlight. Quickly she walked down the porch past the other office doors. Most were labeled with the names of the researchers currently using them; some were marked as all-purpose rooms, shared by everyone.

Vainly searching for a sign showing her where the storage room would be, Elizabeth paced faster down the shaded porch. With her attention riveted so intently on the signs, she almost bumped into her roommate, Clare, just as the young woman stepped out of one of the offices.

"Hey, Elizabeth, it looks like you're in a hurry," the blond Canadian greeted her cheerfully.

"Hi, Clare." Elizabeth stopped and glanced nervously back the way she had come. He was nowhere in sight.

"How's it going with Burk? Are you having a good first day?"

It'll be a good day as long as he doesn't make it my last, she thought cynically. "Dr. Sutherland is a very interesting person to work for." She silently congratulated herself on thinking of something neutral to say.

"Isn't he though," Clare professed, rolled her blue eyes dreamily. "I've been having trouble keeping my mind on my work ever since I caught sight of him."

Elizabeth's eyebrows rose in alarm. She hadn't intended to evoke this kind of response from Clare. The last thing she wanted to do was stand around and discuss Dr. Sutherland with someone who found him attractive. And for it to be Clare, of all people! She had impressed Elizabeth as a serious scholar, definitely not someone whose head could be easily turned by a man with a magnificent body.

Once again she glanced back in the direction of Dr. Sutherland's office. It was so easy to picture how well he filled out his shirt, how the muscles rippled up and down his arms as he painstakingly brushed soil away from his finds at the dig earlier that morning. Elizabeth felt heat rise to her face.

"I mean the guys back home in Montreal are good looking, but . . ." Clare shook her head. "Burk Sutherland is something else. Don't you agree?"

"Oh," Elizabeth frantically searched her mind for some way to change the subject. "I don't know what you mean." She regretted the lie the moment it left her lips.

Clare's eyes opened wide as she stared in disbelief at Elizabeth. "But you've been stuck in that tiny office with him since noon." She laid out the facts as if they should be plain enough for anyone to see.

"I suppose so," Elizabeth reluctantly agreed. "But we've been busy. I've been learning a new job, and Dr. Sutherland can be very demanding, you know."

"I see." Clare arched her brows doubtfully. "But you couldn't have missed noticing his powerful shoulders, could you? And the way his chest muscles flex when he's working on something at the dig?"

"Well, we did spend the morning at the dig, but I was too busy to notice any—"

"But how could you help it? He's so, so big!"

Elizabeth's eyes grew rounder as Clare continued. She felt her pulse throbbing in her right temple, and flicked her gaze around to make sure they were alone. The idea of anyone overhearing their conversation was intolerable. If word of this ever got back to Dr. Sutherland, she knew she would die!

"Is he?" She loaded her voice with the best casual tone she could manage.

"Oh yes." Clare nodded her head vigorously. "Can you

imagine how it would feel to have those strong arms wrapped around you? Heaven," she sighed. "Sheer heaven."

"I suppose so," Elizabeth agreed. Burk was such an intimidating man, she doubted if any woman ever would be able to feel comfortable in his arms. "But we really did work rather hard this morning, and this afternoon will probably be no different. Anyway," Elizabeth continued before Clare could make any further comment about Dr. Sutherland, "I'm on my way to the supply room. Would you happen to know where that is?"

"Sure I do. It's back the other way," she pointed behind Elizabeth, back in the direction of Dr. Sutherland's office. "At that end of the building, it's the last door."

Elizabeth's heart sank. She would have to walk right by his open door. He must have realized when she went hurrying down the porch that she had no idea where she was going. That light bulb was turning into a real problem.

"Thanks, Clare." Elizabeth mustered up a smile for her roommate as she waved goodbye. Reluctantly she turned back in the direction she had come.

"But don't you think it would help me do a better job if I knew a little more about the book you're working on, Dr. Sutherland?" Elizabeth crouched lower by the man as he carefully brushed sediment away from a bone instrument partially buried in the dark earth.

"I honestly don't see how it would make any difference one way or the other. All I expect of you is some simple typing."

She knew she shouldn't let his words hurt her, but they

did. In the few days she had been working with him, his view of her had never wavered. What he didn't say was, in his opinion she wasn't capable of more than "simple typing."

"And could you please call me Burk? I'm tired of looking over my shoulder for my father." He managed to glare a little less harshly this time, she noted. Maybe he was warming up to her after all.

"Your father's a doctor?"

"A surgeon," he replied absently, his attention focused on the artifact he worked to uncover. "In Philadelphia."

"What kind of surgery does he do?"

Burk pulled the brush away from his delicate task and arched his brows at her. "Could we chat later? I have work to do here," he huffed, then returned to his labor.

No, he was definitely not warming up to her. "I can see you're working, Burk." Determined not to let him keep brushing her aside like a bothersome gnat, Elizabeth leaned closer. "Do you plan to uncover the rest of that awl before taking a break? The sun's going to hit this spot in about an—"

Burk was staring up at her, his mouth gaping in surprise.

"What?" she demanded, his baffled expression unnerving her. "What did I do now?"

"How do you know this is an awl?" He straightened from his awkward crouched position, eyeing her sternly. "Do you know what an awl is?"

She sat back on her heels, returning his glare and adding a hint of suspicion to hers. Of course she could identify an awl. Why would he question her like this? He knew her education, he knew her experience at the American Museum of Natural History in New York. There should be no reason for him to be surprised by her identifying an awl when more than half of it sat uncovered already.

Unless he hadn't even bothered to read her application. Could he be so dissatisfied with her getting the job that he hadn't gone to the trouble of finding out what her qualifications were? Why hadn't Wally warned her about the extent of Burk's opposition to her having the job?

"An awl," she fought to hide her swirling emotions, "is a tool that was used in weaving, before needles were available."

"How do you know that?" His tone held a ring of confusion.

Her back stiffened in defense as he stared at her, as if he were accusing her of tricking him. "Everybody knows that," she replied in a falsely casual tone. Now that she had him seemingly off balance, she moved on the offensive. "Now what were you telling me about your book?"

"Well, I . . . It's an overview of the peoples who've inhabited this escarpment. The plains region that runs down the center of the Texas panhandle, about 200 miles long, by about 100 miles wide."

"How far back in history do you plan to cover in the book?" she asked, thrilled that he was willing to answer questions that had been pestering her since her arrival.

"It's going to go all the way back." His face lost its scowl as Burk launched into a subject obviously dear to him. "All the way back to the Paleo-Indian Period, about 11,500 years ago. I've started it with the first people of that period, the Clovis people." Burk hunched over again, returning to his work. "And it's going forward through history, covering four periods, ending with the Garza people of the Protohistoric Period, about 500 years ago.''

He glanced up at Elizabeth, waving his brush occasionally for emphasis. ''I'll put everything in the context of how it relates to the different cultures that moved through this region.''

He smiled, really smiled, and looked right at her when he did it. Elizabeth felt her pulse quicken and she absorbed his words, entranced by each one. His smoky eyes shone so magnificently, as if they were lit from within, as he spoke to her. She smiled back, mesmerized by the deep, resonant tones of his voice. What a wonderful lecturer he must be, the kind of speaker who could keep his audience hanging on every word, just as she was now.

''Was that before the Spanish explorers came through here?'' she asked, prompting him for more information.

''Yes. I'm ending it before their arrival. But if you want to hear more about that era, talk to Ned. He's working on the Spanish influx in the region.''

Ask Ned? What would be the point when there was enough right here to keep her interest forever? ''It will be a fascinating book. I think the extent of the subject matter is perfect,'' she said.

''Do you?'' He looked expectantly up at her, pleasure plain to see on his handsome face.

Sincerely she nodded, smiling back at the enigmatic man she realized she knew almost nothing about. On that first day, that awful day, Elizabeth thought she had him all figured out. In the few days that followed, nothing had happened to change her opinion of Burk Sutherland. Until now, that is.

There was more to him than she ever expected from the grunts of disapproval and glares of tension she had been receiving from him. Also, there was something about him, something familiar about the way he handled himself. He was a man well in command of his life and his environment. She watched him here, and in his office, taking charge of situations, making decisions without hesitation, fully confident in his actions each time.

So masterful, he reminded her of someone. Elizabeth rocked back on her heels, a frown pulling at the corners of her mouth. It was Trevor Davis, her fiancé. Burk reminded her of Trevor, a man on his way up in the financial world. She shook her head, trying to clear it of the confusing images of Trevor. This was the first time in days that her thoughts had rolled around to him, and Elizabeth found them vaguely disturbing.

"How are you dividing the time periods in the book?" She had to keep him talking, to get her mind off Trevor, but also, because she truly wanted to know more about Burk and his work.

Unaware of her inner turmoil, he launched into a fuller explanation of the project that claimed so much of his time, glancing at Elizabeth occasionally as he grew more animated. "The Paleo-Indian Period will fill about half the book." He spoke to her now as an equal. "There were four distinct cultures that inhabited this area then, and I want to define each one."

"And you're starting with the Clovis people?" The conversation flowed easily now. Elizabeth realized they were at a turning point in their relationship, an easing of tensions.

And, as she had hoped, his earlier resentment toward her seemed to fade away.

The air in Burk's office grew sultry as they worked. He rose and turned on the large ceiling fan, then opened the office door. A cool breeze wafted in, driving out the stuffiness that was now bothering them both.

"That's better." Elizabeth sighed in gratification, leaning back from her work to ease her shoulders. She had been typing nonstop since arriving from her hasty lunch in the small kitchen shared by researchers and students alike. "Did you have lunch in here, as usual?"

Since the easing of tension between them that morning, Burk now managed to respond to her idle chatting with civilized answers. But there was no sign of him lessening the hectic pace that he set on her first day here. He always ate lunch at his desk, while pouring over the stacks of papers he seemed to be adding to each day.

"What? Oh. Yes." His attention was already focused back on the illustrations spread across his desk.

Rising to stretch her muscles, Elizabeth peered across the wide desk top at the sketches. "These are great," she commented. "Who did them?"

Burk tugged absently at his lower lip. "I did these. Most of them several weeks ago," he added.

"You?" Her eyebrows, a shade darker than her hair, rose high in surprise.

He spared her a quick grin. "I'm a pretty competent technical illustrator."

Elizabeth laughed lightly, shaking her loose hair back over her shoulders. How very like Burk, she mused. So confident in his abilities, and so accepting of himself. Burk Sutherland wasn't bragging when he said he could do something well. It was simply a fact of his life that he took in stride. He had no need to crow about his talents, or accomplishments. Also, Elizabeth could certainly see, he wasn't a man who would ever rest on his laurels.

Burk was a man of action. Even as they spoke he continued to sort the illustrations, checking and double-checking the skillful labeling he had been doing. Elizabeth watched in fascination as he singled out a sketch and placed it on the tidy drafting table adjoining his desk.

"But I'm not much of a photographer," he said, pointing to a stack of glossy pictures on a corner of his desk.

Elizabeth picked them up and thumbed through the prints. "Uh, well, they're not bad." She tried to be encouraging, but even to her untrained eye the pictures looked dull and lifeless.

"Gee, thanks." He flashed her a wide grin. "But honestly, those are just prints I'm using for ideas. Ned is doing the real photography for my book."

"Oh, that's great."

"And I'm doing the illustrations for his project. Kind of an exchange thing." He dipped his head in the direction of the wooden shelf near her desk. "The ones Ned did are over there."

With a quick glimpse of the top photo Elizabeth was able to tell the difference. "These are great!" she exclaimed.

"Yes, Ned's good. He really knows what he's doing."

"And so do you," she said, crossing the room again to stand behind him. "What're you doing to that drawing?" She stretched across the desk to get a better look at the

drawing of a mammoth, with its curling tusks, foraging across a quiet landscape.

"I'm labeling the different types of food sources in the illustration. I don't like to do any labeling until I've got the picture just the way I want it."

Suddenly aware of her arm brushing against Burk's, Elizabeth straightened up. Her breathing had grown slightly deeper, and she forced herself to relax. This was silly! There was no reason to act like a schoolgirl around this man. He was an intensely dedicated scientist, not some hormone-driven teen. Elizabeth forced herself to watch his movements, warning herself that this was Dr. Burk Sutherland, her boss.

After selecting another pen from his drawer, Burk tested it on a blank sheet of paper. When he felt satisfied, he began meticulously filling in the names of various plants. He executed the lettering with machine precision.

Elizabeth watched intently for a moment, until she felt her breathing return to normal, then left him to his labors. Thank goodness he hadn't noticed her silly reaction, she mused while wandering back toward her typing table. The sound of laughter drifting through the open door caught her attention. Drawn to it, she stepped outside.

A small group of people, dressed for a casual evening out in the city, were making their way from the low dorm buildings up the unpaved path to the parking lot. She caught sight of her Canadian roommate, Clare, among them. It looked as if they were all having such a good time, Elizabeth mused.

They were doing exactly what she had come here to do. Each one, leaving their responsibilities behind, going out

to have a little fun. Elizabeth imagined it would be an evening of casual conversation, good food, and fun entertainment. They would be doing it in what she had always heard was one of the friendliest states in America. Out among Texans, known far and wide for their easy smiles and genuine hospitality.

Enviously, Elizabeth stared at their backs, knowing that she could have been with them. Earlier that morning, Clare had invited her to come with the group, assuring her that she would be welcome among the friendly coworkers.

Knowing Burk's schedule, she had reluctantly refused. There was no chance that he would be through working before dark. A couple of nights he had kept her working until midnight.

Glancing, disheartened, behind her, Elizabeth studied the intense set of Burk's posture as he diligently worked on the illustrations. "Will we be working late this evening?"

"Hmm?" Burk glanced up briefly. "Oh, I suppose so," he answered absently, his attention still riveted on the drawing.

Now she fully understood how driven, how motivated he was to produce this book that meant so much to him. The dedication and drive he possessed were two traits that she recognized as rare. Traits that she should admire in him. But just for a little while, just for one evening, she wished he would quit work early. If he would let her have an evening free to do whatever she wanted to, it would mean so much to her.

Elizabeth peered back out the door, catching a glimpse of sunlight reflecting off a window as cars left the parking lot. She felt a pang of loneliness as the sky grew darker.

Turning away from the brilliant sunset and thoughts of the people on their way to the city, Elizabeth went back inside. Her only company for the evening would be a man so lost in his work that he hardly knew she was there.

"Three days, Clare." Elizabeth spun around in the dorm room with delight. "Three whole days of no digging, no typing, nothing but freedom." After two weeks of nonstop work, Elizabeth felt more than ready for a break.

"I'm glad you're so happy about the guys leaving on this research trip, Elizabeth," Clare lamented. "But I had planned to ask Ned out this weekend." Clare flopped down across her narrow bed in the Spartan room she and Elizabeth shared.

"You were?" Disbelief flashed in Elizabeth's eyes.

"Yes," her roommate pouted. "We usually go out with the gang on Saturdays, and I thought I'd ask him to have a drink with me first. Then we'd join up with everybody and go dancing as usual."

"But Clare, isn't he a bit old for you?"

"Of course not. He's only two years older than Burk."

Elizabeth shot her a derisive look. "Is that supposed to make me feel better?"

"Burk's only thirty-two," Clare said with a note of strained patience.

Feeling her brows shoot up in surprise, Elizabeth quickly masked her expression. "You mean he's only eight years older than me?"

"Uh-huh. And in my book that seems just about perfect."

"But he seems so much older," she sputtered. "Burk

acts so . . . he treats me so . . .'' At a loss for words, she shook her head. "I'll never figure him out," she huffed.

The blonde Canadian rolled over on her side and stared keenly at Elizabeth. "At least you're finally calling Burk by his first name. I didn't think things would ever ease up between you two."

"Was it that obvious that we weren't getting along at first?"

"Only a little," Clare reassured her. "But things are going okay now, aren't they?"

"Yes. But I'm still grateful for these three days away from him. The hectic pace he keeps is beginning to wear me down."

There was another reason nagging at the back of her mind. She was becoming too aware of Dr. Burk Sutherland. It seemed impossible to turn around in that small office without almost stumbling over him.

Being his assistant required her to be with him all day long. There were never any significant stretches of time when the two of them weren't together, and she was beginning to realize that he was taking up more and more time in her private thoughts too.

She needed this weekend to get her mind clear of Burk Sutherland.

"Let's get ready." Elizabeth threw open the closet door and rummaged through her clothes. "The cookout at the compound starts in less than an hour, and I'm sure it'll take both our minds off our troubles."

"You're probably right." Clare sighed as she drew herself up from the bed. "I need a distraction. Something to get my thoughts off Ned."

Elizabeth silently agreed. A distraction was just what she needed tonight too.

"That's the spirit," she quipped. "We need a little celebration, and it's going to be a blast having a cookout around a real campfire tonight."

"You seem awfully happy about this, Elizabeth. It almost sounds as if you've never been to a cookout before."

Clare turned and rummaged through her drawers, quickly pulling out shorts and blouses, and just as quickly stuffing them back in.

"I haven't," Elizabeth admitted with a slight shrug.

"Really?" Clare's eyes were wide with amazement. "Never?"

Elizabeth laughed at her friend's honest reaction. "Never. Manhattan isn't exactly the ideal setting for cookouts, I suppose. And my friends back home aren't quite the 'outdoors' type."

"But don't you live across from Central Park? Surely you must go there a lot."

"No. Not really." She didn't want to admit there were few enough times that she could count all of them on one hand. Her parents always discouraged activities that weren't strictly ladylike, and Elizabeth never went against their wishes. Until the time she took archaeology classes in college, she thought ruefully. Even then, she managed to hide her class schedule from them until her graduation.

"But I plan to spend a lot of time outside while I'm here in Texas," she declared. "As much time as I can."

"You need to lay the law down to Burk when he gets back." Clare shook a warning finger at her. "He's got to stop taking advantage of you like he has. Tell him you refuse to work those long hours.''

How Elizabeth wished she could! If she could march up to him and demand he give her the free time she so desperately wanted. . . . That had been one of her main reasons for coming here in the first place. But Elizabeth couldn't imagine herself giving Burk Sutherland any kind of ultimatum. He was simply too imperious, too strong for her to ever stand up against.

He was so much like Trevor.

Chapter Three

"We'll leave in the morning at five, Elizabeth. Be sure you're ready," Burk instructed her as he searched through the papers on his desk. He had been going at a mad pace since returning with Ned two days ago.

"But why do you need me along? I could stay here," she suggested. "I could type up whatever notes you brought back from your trip with Ned."

"Impossible," he declared. "There would be nothing for you to do. I spent so much time riding in the jeep that I managed to organize my notes and condense them down to the few paragraphs I'll need for the book." Burk pulled a topographic map from the pile of papers he had been rummaging through. "The trip went so well, we managed to complete everything I wanted done on the western border of the escarpment. Now it's time to finish the Caprock formation along the eastern border."

"That's marvelous, Burk." She followed his finger as

he traced along the lines of the map, down the jagged eastern edge of the escarpment, pausing at the Lubbock Lake Site. "But I don't understand. What good will it do to take me along? Isn't there something I could do here?"

Elizabeth searched his suntanned face as he studied the map, letting her eyes linger on his smoky gray ones. He must have been out in the sun a great deal during the three days they were apart. A roseyness lit his cheeks. It was a flush put there by the bright Texas sun.

Allowing her gaze to wander upward, she noticed his hair looked more tousled than usual. She could easily imagine what he looked like out there, high on the edge of those cliffs, buffeted by the strong breeze that constantly swept across the wide range of the plains.

Burk was a man who fit well in the landscape of the rolling plains. His eyes were the color of the puffy gray clouds that scudded along beneath the great expanses of rolling white thunderheads of the broad Texas skies.

The sky here was so vast. Days ago, she and Clare spent an entire afternoon lying in the sun, and that was the first time the Texas sky had captured her heart. She could never remember seeing a sky so immense before. Clare soon grew tired of hearing her endless comments about it, and jokingly suggested that their next outing would have to be something more exciting.

A day in the close confines of a tiny jeep with Burk would certainly be interesting, but Elizabeth could hardly call the idea exciting.

"I promise that it won't be too boring," Burk said as he arched one brow at her.

A flush of embarrassment colored her cheeks. Could he have read her mind? "I . . . I don't know what you mean—"

"I realize it must sound dull, riding around all day in a stuffy jeep with two stodgy old archaeologists. But I think we could get a lot done on organizing the general look of the last half of the book."

"Stodgy and old?" Her mouth tightened into a thin line of disapproval.

"I know it'll be tedious for you, stuck with an old—"

"Dr. Sutherland, I happen to know that you're thirty-two years old. And if you'd bothered to read my application you'd know that I'm only eight years younger than you."

Irritation glinted in Elizabeth's eyes, but she immediately regretted the words. She hadn't intended to confront him about her suspicions. Since her first day here she'd harbored the notion that he hadn't even taken the time to read her application, that he was unhappy with the fact that she had this job. Why hadn't Wally warned her, she wondered for the tenth time.

"You're twenty-four? I thought you were . . . There must be an error on your—"

"There is no error, Dr. Sutherland. I typed that form myself, and, as you're well aware, I happen to be a very good typist."

"Miss Way—"

"After all, how do you think I got this job?" Elizabeth pressed her palms to her burning cheeks. So, it's back to Dr. Sutherland, and Miss Way, is it? The easy camaraderie that took so long to develop between them quickly boiled away into steam in the heat of her anger. She balled her hands and forced them to her sides.

Burk sat down heavily at his desk, staring at this wildcat in front of him. How could things deteriorate so quickly? One minute she was quiet, little Elizabeth, and the next, Miss Way, the bane of his existence.

"I just meant..." What did he mean? That she's too young to find his work interesting? Had he really been saying something that insulting? No wonder she took offense. Age shouldn't enter into it, he realized.

But he thought of her as much younger than twenty-four. He felt sure that her application listed her age as younger than that. Much younger. Across the room sat the filing cabinet where he'd jammed the letter and application from the Archaeology Institute. The letter informed him of Elizabeth's getting the job as his new assistant. He should pull the letter out, right now, and see if he was crazy or not.

Looking back up at Elizabeth he saw the hurt hiding in her face behind the flush of anger. No, he couldn't do it to her. He couldn't bear the thought of causing her any more pain than his thoughtlessness already had.

"I'm sorry. That was unforgivably rude of me." His eyes clouded with remorse as he gazed up at her flushed face. "It slipped my mind that you're close to my age. You look so much younger, you see." He fumbled for words, trying to give her one of those disarming grins Ned used on so many females. But to Burk, it felt more like a grimace.

The reaction to his attempt at a disarming grin wasn't what he wished for. Elizabeth's eyes twitched wider. Then she covered her face with her slim hands and spun away from him, leaving him staring at her back. He focused on the lustrous fall of chestnut hair sweeping over her shoulders. It ended in a straight line a few inches below her collar. Thick and gleaming, it was all one length, and she had it gathered back from her face by a bright red band.

Burk leaned across his desk and reached out a hand to stroke its shimmering softness, to comfort her. He wanted to take away the bitter feelings that had surfaced and come between them. A strong need burned in him to tell her he hadn't meant to hurt her. Suddenly, it was very important that she realize he hadn't meant to allow anything to come between them.

His hand paused inches from her hair. Her shoulders were shaking. He had made her cry.

As she turned back around to face him, he quickly dropped his outstretched hand to the cluttered desk top. Her slender fingers began wiping tears from her eyes, but she was laughing. Silent laughter shook her chestnut hair, sending sparkles of light dancing through its compelling abundance.

"I can't . . . " She paused to catch her breath. "I can't believe I snapped at you for thinking I look younger than I am. My mother would practically kill to be insulted like that."

Like spreading wildfire her laughter reached him and instantly brought a smile to his lips. Burk tilted his head back and joined her, laughing loud and long. All the frustration and irritation he felt during the last month eased its hard grip on his chest as he laughed. Delight took its place as he watched her wipe more drops of moisture from her coal-dark lashes.

What would it feel like to reach up and brush her lashes

dry himself? Would they be as velvety soft as they looked? Would she pull back? He couldn't risk it, couldn't chance seeing the rejection that might appear in her eyes. Not now, when these feelings were still so new.

Giving himself a little mental shake, Burk cleared his throat and pulled his eyes away from the enchanting picture Elizabeth made. Picking up the map, he searched for the markings of the route they would travel tomorrow.

A whimsical smile still tugged at the corners of his lips as he launched into an explanation of his plans. "This is the eastern boundary, where the Caprock formation runs north and south."

"Like a long cliff," Elizabeth observed.

"Yes, broken by an occasional stream that's eroded it down to a slope. We're going to this point of erosion. It's called Mulberry Canyon."

"And this blue line?"

"That's one of the creeks that join east of here to form the Red River. What I'm most interested in is the cliff face of the canyon. With this part facing due east, we should be able to get some decent pictures of the cliff were the erosion is minor."

"So we have to be there by dawn?" Elizabeth looked up into his eyes doubtfully.

Burk smiled sympathetically at her. "Ned says it'll be best if we are."

"Well," she arched her brows and gave him a half-hearted smile, "I'm game if you are, Burk."

So they were back on a first name basis, he realized. Things were turning out all right, after all. "Let's get these papers packed up in that box," he pointed behind her at a

small, cardboard box by the door. "You'll also need a pen
or two, Elizabeth."

He watched her collect the box and pens, admiring the
way she moved with efficient, sure grace, just as she always
did. Even during those first days when he was being so
abrupt with her, he remembered with a wave of embarrassment.

How in the world could he ever have thought that this
lovely young woman got the job because her boyfriend
gave it to her? Vividly, he replayed the words she had just
spoken in such irritation when she asked how he thought
she got the job. If she had been able to read his mind at
that moment, there probably would have been no way to
salvage this relationship. It would have been impossible for
them to work together if she knew what he had suspected
until he learned that Wally was a family friend, and not her
boyfriend.

Burk busied himself gathering the papers they would use
during their long drive tomorrow. But his gaze kept wandering back to Elizabeth. Since Wally wasn't her boyfriend,
he wondered, who was?

"Will you be needing any of your files from in here?"
she asked, indicating a gray metal cabinet.

"No," he answered hastily. That was the cabinet he had
been eyeing earlier. The one that held her application, and
the letter from Wally. "Nothing from inside, just the blue
book on top, thanks."

Trying to picture the application in his mind, Burk
watched Elizabeth place the book he indicated in the box.
Thinking back on it now, he was sure the blanks on that

form were filled in with a pen. He felt sure of it. But Elizabeth insisted that she had typed it.

Burk took a step toward the cabinet, then stopped himself. He couldn't check on it with Elizabeth here. It would have to wait till they got back from the trip tomorrow afternoon, when he could take a look at it while she was out of the office.

"We're almost there, Elizabeth," Burk said as he reached back and gently patted her arm.

The quiet conversation between Burk and Ned in the front seats of the jeep managed to keep her awake only till the city lights of Lubbock faded into the night. She quickly fell asleep in the back as Ned drove the jeep through the dark countryside during the still hours before dawn.

"What time is it?" she asked, her voice scratchy with sleep.

"Almost six. It'll be dawn by the time we stop."

A warm glow tinged the rim of the eastern sky, she saw. Sitting up straighter, Elizabeth pushed her chestnut hair from her face, and peered out at their dark surroundings. The country was still treeless, rolling plains as far as she could see in all directions. But soon they would reach the point where the earth seemed to break off and plummet down, to settle at the base of a long cliff. There, it would be just as flat and treeless as the upper part.

"Where's the canyon?" she asked, squinting through the darkness, unable to find any sign of their destination.

"Just a few miles ahead," Burk reassured her. "We'll

be coming up to the top of the northeast cliff in a few minutes.''

Elizabeth shoved her feet back into her shoes, and ran a brush through the riotous tangle of her hair. As Ned turned from the main highway onto a narrow dirt road, she glanced briefly at Burk's strong profile. The dash lights glinted off the angular planes of his features, revealing the serious set of his lips.

What an intimate moment it had been when he reached back and nudged her awake. His voice sounded so velvety soft when he spoke her name, she almost thought she was dreaming. Had he been in her dreams? Yes, she was shocked to realize.

Burk Sutherland had been there, standing in the clear sunlight at the dig, giving her a lecture on the different uses of bone awls. And she sat on the ground, busily typing every word he said on an old manual typewriter. It looked just like one she had seen in an antique shop she had visited with Clare during that three-day break.

But something about the dream bothered her. She remembered a shadowy figure of a man standing beside her, someone whose face she couldn't quite remember. At some point during the lecture, that person stepped in front of her, blocking her view of Burk. Elizabeth remembered trying to get him to move aside, but the stranger ignored her, keeping his back turned to her. She'd reached up, tugging on the dark jacket of his well-tailored suit. When he turned to knock her hand away, she realized it was Trevor, her fiancé.

The memory of the shock she had felt brought a blanch of pain to her features. With an effort, she formed them into a mask of calmness just as Burk turned back to her and smiled.

"There's the sun," he said as he pointed out the window. Then he ran his restless fingers through his wild shock of hair, leaving it as rumpled as Elizabeth felt hers must look after spending half the night sleeping in the back of a jeep.

This experience exhilarated her, she realized. But it wasn't hard to imagine the horrified look her mother would have on her face if she ever learned of what Elizabeth was doing right now. She smiled at the image that thought brought to mind, and found she was echoing Burk's look of excitement.

In the growing light of dawn, their gazes locked for a moment. It was the first time Elizabeth could remember ever sharing a moment with Burk that wasn't totally related to work, in one aspect or another.

A quiet thrill flowed through her as Burk rested his smoky eyes on her.

"This is it, guys." Ned's voice shattered the quiet connection they shared as he brought the jeep to a stop.

Outside her window, Elizabeth saw a dark ending of the ground, a void, just yards from where Ned had stopped. It truly looked as if the Earth broke off at that point, but in the distance to the east, she could see bands of light reflecting back from the ground far below.

Burk and Ned stepped out, and Elizabeth scrambled to join them on the rim of the canyon. Diffuse rays of sunlight filtered through a low band of clouds, blue with haze. Soon, the red ball would be high enough to light the canyon and reveal it's hidden wonders, and she would see it all for the first time at Burk's side.

"We're on a little triangle of land that sticks out into the lowland," Burk informed her, standing there with his hands clasped behind his back.

The perfect lecturer's pose, she reflected. Perfect, like everything that Burk Sutherland did.

"From here, we should be able to get all the pictures necessary," he continued.

"I can take a hint," Ned chided his friend, and returned to the jeep for his equipment.

She stood alone in the growing light with Burk, enjoying the sunrise. "How high up are we?"

"This spot is about 3200 feet, another thousand feet higher than the land out there," Burk replied, indicating the vast expanse stretching east of them.

"I feel like I'm standing on top of the world. But it's so different than standing on top of a mountain. When I was in finishing school in Switzerland I went on a trip to Mont Blanc once. We rode to the top of the mountain in one of those unusual cogwheel trains." She paused to look up at Burk and was startled to discover him gazing so intently at her. Before she could continue she had to look away, back at the canyon. "It's much higher, but the view was nothing like this."

Quietly, he stepped closer to her. "Tell me about it. What strikes you as so different about this view?"

"It's . . . so open, so limitless. I feel like I can almost see back to the Atlantic Ocean." She glanced furtively up at him. "I must sound silly," she declared.

"No, not at all," he assured her, bringing his arms from behind his back.

Elizabeth stared at the strong hands she spent so many

hours watching at the dig. Unconsciously, she took a small step closer to him. How would it feel to have his arm around her? What if he just casually laid an arm across her shoulder, so he could point out a feature in the distance that he wanted her to see? She could ask him about something out there, couldn't she?

Scanning the canyon floor for something to talk about, Elizabeth refused to allow herself to contemplate her motives at the moment. She simply wanted to know what it would feel like to have Burk Sutherland's arm around her, even if only for a moment.

"Over here, you two," Ned called, startling her back to reality.

What had she been thinking? Burk was a scientist, here to do a job, not some lovestruck boy on a late-night date. Squaring her shoulders, she marched to the spot where Ned had set up his tripod. The two men soon busied themselves checking reference points on the map.

"We should get a few pictures here," Burk decided. "Then move on east to the point of the triangle. I think that spot will show the cliff face and the canyon floor well, with the sun's illumination."

"Sounds good to me," Ned agreed.

"Elizabeth, I'll go back to the jeep and sketch a few details, if you'll help Ned with his equipment," Burk suggested.

She wanted to say no. She wanted to go back to the jeep and help him. But there didn't seem to be any valid reason to do so, not that she could think of. So she stayed on the cliff edge, but her eyes followed Burk.

"That's it," Ned exclaimed.

"What?" Elizabeth looked at him in bewilderment.

"I'm done," he shrugged his shoulders as he pulled the camera off the tripod. "I've gotten all the pictures Burk needs."

"So soon?"

"Soon?" he asked, arching a brow at her. "We've been working in this spot for almost half an hour. Aren't you ready to go?"

Had it been that long? Could her attention have been directed at Burk so intently, she hadn't been aware of the passage of time? A blush of embarrassment colored her cheeks as she turned to help Ned get the equipment back to the jeep.

"Ah," Burk exclaimed in satisfaction as he saw them approaching. "Let's get out to the point of the canyon wall. I want to be sure we get all the pictures today."

"Don't worry, Burk. We'll make it." Ned grinned at his zealous friend.

The sun wasn't far from the eastern horizon by the time Ned was back at work again. Elizabeth sat on a boulder nearby, staring off into the deep canyon. From her vantage point she could see Burk also. He knelt on the ground a few feet from the jeep and seemed deeply absorbed in sketching the canyon spread majestically before them.

"This is marvelous, Burk," Ned called out. "We could never have gotten a view like this anywhere else without renting a helicopter."

"That's true," Burk heartily agreed. "But don't take any chances on that edge there. I don't trust that crumbling rock."

Ned grinned wryly and took a small step away from the edge.

"That goes for you too, Elizabeth." Burk glanced up long enough to shake his pencil at her.

Burk was worried about her, actually worried about her safety. Such an odd feeling, she realized, to have a man worry about her. Trevor never voiced any concern about her safety. The only thing Trevor was ever concerned about seemed to be the business deal he was currently working on.

Of course there was that one time at the opera. Trevor had gotten very upset when her dress got ruined. A man had stumbled into her in the lobby and splashed white wine all over her satin gown. Trevor made the slightly tipsy man apologize, and then tucked her in a cab and sent her home.

At that moment, she felt cared for, she remembered, but it certainly wasn't the same feeling she was experiencing right now. Burk's casual warning about the danger of the crumbling edge strangely meant more to her than every instance of concern Trevor had ever shown her.

"I won't be going any closer to the edge than this," Elizabeth assured him. "I wouldn't want to distract you from your work."

"Oh?" He arched one brow mischievously at her. "Are you sure it's not because you're afraid of heights?"

"Me? Of course not," she retorted.

"Well, I know I am," he announced, then shifted his gaze to the tablet in his lap.

Afraid of heights? Was he serious? Elizabeth studied the man as his brow furrowed. He concentrated on his sketch, and she realized his thoughts were already buried in his work. He was so driven, so motivated to succeed. Idly she wondered what drove him on so.

Trevor's motivation was power and money. But what did Burk Sutherland want? What made him devote all his time to his work? A pure love of archaeology, she suspected.

A scraping sound brushed against the edge of her awareness, drawing her attention away from Burk, toward the cliff.

Ned had slipped down to one knee, and was wobbling over the edge of the cliff! As if she was moving in slow motion, Elizabeth screamed and leaped from her perch on the boulder.

Burk snapped his head around to her, instantly assessing the situation and understanding the source of her fright. Dropping his sketch pad, he leaped toward Ned, but his fingers closed on emptiness.

Ned disappeared over the side, without a sound. Elizabeth felt the air thicken about her as she fought her way against rebelling muscles to the cliff edge, where Burk lay prone.

"Hold on, Ned!"

"What?" Elizabeth dropped to the ground beside Burk and peered over the dizzying edge into the vast canyon. Ned hung from the vertical wall a few yards below them. Somehow, he had managed to hook his fingers over a small outcropping of rock, and now hung on for his life.

"Hold on, buddy," Burk called to his friend. "I'll get you out of this."

"Yeah," Ned weakly replied.

Without a moment's hesitation Burk slid a few feet to his left and swung his tall frame over the side.

"Burk!" Elizabeth cried in horror. "What are you doing?"

"What I have to," he calmly replied. "Now move away from that spot, you'll knock dirt and rocks off onto Ned."

With those parting words, Burk's unruly thatch of hair disappeared from her view. A terrible clenching sensation gripped Elizabeth's stomach as she rocked back onto her heels. Wringing her hands together, she glanced frantically about for any sign of help. There was no one else in sight. No houses, cars, or people that she could run to for help. Ned hung there, in danger of plunging to his death, and Burk seemed determined to follow him.

Unable to bear the suspense, Elizabeth scooted to her right, well away from Ned and Burk, and peered over the cliff. Ned still hung in the same position, motionless and straining to keep his tenuous grip.

Burk searched for grips and toeholds in the fractured face of the cliff. Centuries of erosion on the eastern face of the plateau had worn away the soil to expose rocks and small crevices. Burk took advantage of each one as he slowly worked his way to Ned.

"I can see your way out now." Burk's deep voice rang clear in the morning air. He stretched one hand out and grasped Ned's right wrist. "I'll pull you up about a foot, then you'll be able to get a toehold. When I say 'now.' Ready?"

"Yeah," Ned answered, more strongly this time.

"Now!" Burk heaved as Ned stretched and caught a handhold and his foot found the outcropping Burk hoped it would.

"Okay, there's another handhold just to your right,"

Burk said as he released his grip on Ned. "That's it, a little higher now."

Ned moved as Burk instructed him to, never balking, never protesting as his friend guided him over inch by inch to the cliff face where Burk had descended from the canyon rim. Elizabeth dug her fingers into the soil, straining with each move the men made on their climb back to the top.

As Burk boosted Ned over the edge, Elizabeth scrambled forward and pulled the shaken man to safety. She eased Ned down and turned back as Burk's straining face appeared over the rim. Eagerly, she reached out and pulled on his broad shoulders, steadying him as he climbed back onto the level ground and collapsed next to Ned.

"You both could have been killed!" Elizabeth's voice quavered as she stared down into Burk's gray eyes.

Fine beads of perspiration glinted on his brow as he reached a scuffed hand up to brush back his tousled hair. "Everything turned out all right, Elizabeth."

She wasn't sure if he was admonishing her or comforting her. Reeling from the emotions that still flooded through her, Elizabeth stared in bewilderment at Burk's ruggedly handsome features. She could still taste the fear she felt when he was in danger. It had almost paralyzed her, the thought of losing this man who sprang into her life with such an undeniable impact.

And now that she had him back on firm ground, all she could bring herself to do was sit there and look into his smoldering eyes, so passionate, so commanding. The shaking in her limbs must be as much from the terror she felt as from the awakening feelings that Burk was beginning to stir in her heart. As she absorbed that fact, Elizabeth's eyes grew rounder.

Chapter Four

As insane as it all seemed to Elizabeth, Burk and Ned never hesitated for a moment before returning to work on the cliff's edge. Although they did manage to stay a healthy distance from the crumbling spot where Ned had stood minutes earlier.

"Don't look so worried," Burk admonished her. "Everything turned out all right, didn't it?"

"You call that 'all right'?" Elizabeth finally managed to find her voice. "Ned almost fell to his death. And you, you tried your hardest to join him!" She stared wild-eyed at Burk, daring him to make that near disaster seem any less dangerous than it had been.

Burk eyed her dubiously, but chose not to argue any further.

Elizabeth wiped trembling hands across her troubled brow, trying to ease the tension that still held her in its grip.

"The sun's just right for these shots, Burk. I'd better get a move on if we want to finish all this in one trip."

"You're right, Ned." Burk turned from Elizabeth and joined Ned. "I don't relish the idea of making a trip back up here again. Can I help you with anything?"

As the two men busied themselves, Elizabeth wheeled around and stormed back to the jeep. She wrenched open the door and clambered up into the front passenger seat. Crossing her arms stiffly over her chest, she glared out the windshield at the beauty of the open terrain spread far below the high escarpment.

How could they act that way? So blasé about almost being killed. Burk Sutherland was as overbearing as he was stubborn, refusing to accept the danger he had placed himself in.

"Let's load up our gear, Elizabeth," Burk called to her, temporarily putting a stop to her fuming. Flinging herself out of the jeep, she stomped toward him, her pace faltering when she realized her steps were imitating Burk's usual style of walking.

"Will you grab my sketch pad?" he asked, pointing to the white paper lying in the patch of grass, right where he dropped it before lunging to the cliff's edge.

Elizabeth remembered how his lithe body strained forward, trying to grasp his falling friend. Clutching her lower lip between her teeth to stop its quivering, Elizabeth hastily scooped up the pad and eyed the sketch.

With masterful strokes, Burk had started a scene depicting a group of people standing on the far cliff across the canyon. From the knowledge she had gained working by

Burk's side so closely, she thought the sketch must be intended for the first half of his book.

"This is sometime during the Paleo-Indian period," she said as she brought the sketch book to the jeep and stood at Burk's shoulder.

"Uh-huh." His reply was short.

"The hunters are carrying spears, and that means they're one of the four groups of people that lived here during that period. But I can't tell which group these are."

"Folsom, the second group." He eyed her more closely as she studied the sketch. "You couldn't tell from that," he indicated the pad in her hands. "I'll set in a large sketch of the spear point in the lower corner of the picture. That'll illustrate one of the differences between the Folsom people and the two groups that followed them during the Paleo-Indian period."

"The Plainview and the Firstview people?"

"Yes. And I'll be almost done with the first half of the book when we get these pictures developed."

"That's everything, folks," Ned announced cheerfully as he closed the back window of the jeep. "Were you planning to sit in back with Elizabeth so the two of you could work on the way back to Lubbock?"

The two of them, sitting in the confining space of the jeep's back seat? The thought of being so close to Burk sent small shivers up Elizabeth's arms. Working side by side at the dig or in Burk's cramped office seemed somehow so different from the idea of sitting in the back seat beside him.

Shifting her gaze up to Burk's serious features, Elizabeth studied the tense set of his shoulders. Burk was so far from the innocent images of the young boys she used to fantasize about. So tall and ruggedly handsome, there almost appeared to be something foreboding about him. The somber expression that covered his face so much of the time was a stark reminder to her that this was no inexperienced boy beside her now. This was a man, with a deep passion for learning and for his work. What would it be like if he ever turned his intensity toward a woman? What if that woman could be her?

How in the world had her thoughts gotten around to that? Heat flushed her face instantly, and Elizabeth ducked her head to hide the redness. Air fluttered in and out of her lungs in little bursts and Elizabeth fought to control her imagination.

Closing the tablet to protect the sketch Burk had begun before Ned's fateful plunge over the cliff, Elizabeth opened the door of the jeep.

"Here, let me help you." Burk stepped up behind her and held out his hand.

After the briefest of hesitations, she accepted his offer. The problem was, she couldn't be sure how it would feel to touch the man she had been fantasizing about only moments before.

And her hesitation proved to be justified. Burk's firm grip on her hand drew Elizabeth's eyes to that point, where his flesh caressed hers. Their palms molded together, their fingers entwined, and the effect on Elizabeth stunned her.

A thudding started in her heart and instantly traveled down to the bare flesh where he touched her. She felt his grasp, felt the strength in his hand, the heat in his fingers. The contact with him set her mind reeling back to the first day when they met outside in the clearing. He was such an enigma to her then. One minute sending an exhilarating coolness through her body with his light touch, and the next, suggesting she quit and go back to New York.

"Thanks," she stammered. What could she say to break the tension that she felt building inside her heart? If his brief touch could do something as profound as this to her, what would it be like to spend the two hours of the drive nestled beside Burk in the narrow back seat of the jeep? Her heart began racing again as she put her foot on the metal step and climbed inside.

The heat of his touch stayed with her as their fingers broke contact. Elizabeth sank gratefully down onto the solid support of the seat.

"It might be a bit too crowded for you if I sat back there, Elizabeth," Burk said.

Could he be as reluctant as she to endure such a close space for the long ride that was ahead of them? His unwavering gaze certainly didn't reflect that. He stood in the open doorway, watching her with an expectant look in his eye.

"You aren't still upset about what happened to Ned, are you?" Burk asked.

It wasn't hard to notice that he made no mention of the danger he'd placed himself in. Or that he'd charged over the side with no hesitation, and risked his own life to save someone else's.

"Elizabeth?" Her name was almost an appeal on his lips. "Everything turned out all right. Ned's not hurt." He spoke softly now.

She couldn't stop it. Her bottom lip quivered, just as her

whole body had when she saw Burk's head disappear over the side of the cliff. She sucked it in and held it still between clenched teeth.

"Elizabeth." Burk leaned in the doorway, placing his hand on her knee.

Fighting to keep the wavering tone from her voice, Elizabeth asked, "And what about you? You could have been killed too. What if you had slipped, missed a handhold? Did you ever stop to think about that?"

A crease appeared on his forehead as his troubled eyebrows drew together. He shook his head. "I knew that Ned couldn't get out of that spot without my help." He shrugged his shoulders, his hand sliding from her knee.

Its absence felt like a rush of icy water across her skin. Elizabeth blankly rubbed the spot where his hand had so tenderly rested. "You could have fallen—" She felt her lip begin to quiver again and bit down on it, hoping he wouldn't realize how very upset she was at the idea of losing him.

Burk leaned close again, but before he could speak, Ned opened the driver's door and got in the jeep.

"Ready to go, folks?"

Burk hastily pulled back his outstretched hand, and brushed his palms against the dusty legs of his tight jeans. "As we'll ever be, Ned," he replied. With one hand on top of the door frame, Burk swung into the front seat and pulled the door closed.

"Weren't you going to sit in the back?" Ned asked, sending a questioning look in Burk's direction.

"I need room to spread my papers out," Elizabeth interjected. "We'll get a lot of work done this way, really," she assured him.

Ned shrugged as he started the jeep and skirted the canyon back to the highway. Elizabeth stared out the back window at the retreating canyon as they made their way back to the highway. The angular ribbon of the cliff face faded from view before the jeep bumped up onto the smooth highway and turned south for the two-hour drive back to the archaeological site.

It must be true. Burk seemed just as uncomfortable as she at the idea of riding in the back seat together. A quiet sigh escaped her lips as Elizabeth searched through the box at her feet for the work she'd brought to do on the trip.

"Could you hand me the blue book? The one you got from on top of the filing cabinet?"

Careful to keep her head down, Elizabeth pulled the book from the box and held it up toward Burk. Somehow, she managed to hold the book by the corner, so their fingers wouldn't brush against each other, but Elizabeth felt oddly disappointed when her plan succeeded. She managed to avoid touching him, but the regret of that missed contact almost troubled her more than the touch of Burk's hand would have. Now, she felt sure of it.

This man was definitely occupying too much of her mind. This silly feeling his presence caused in her stomach, that fluttering sensation, was becoming a real problem. Elizabeth knew that she had to get control of her childish reactions soon, or she wouldn't be able to do her best work with Burk around, and that was something neither he nor she would tolerate.

Briefly, she glanced up at the man who lived at the center

of her thoughts almost all the time lately, and found him looking back at her. A jolt shot through her, and she felt herself sink helplessly into the smoky depth of his eyes. Those incredible eyes, they haunted her dreams.

Burk Sutherland had grown bigger than life during the times she allowed her mind to wander off on fanciful flights of its own. Flights far from the mundane reality of life as his assistant. Her heart asked for more, more from this man who sat within arm's length of her. Her spirit was free of the restraints she placed on herself, free to reach out and take what it wanted, to have Burk Sutherland. To touch him, to caress him, to kiss him.

Unbidden by her conscious thoughts, she saw her hand rise up to stroke his arm. Stunned by the movement, Elizabeth jerked her hand back as if he were a hot flame. Sizzling from the embarrassment she felt flush her face, she tore her eyes from him and reached for her pen and paper. Pulling out a sheaf of notes, she busied herself, trying to organize the work in front of her.

Although trying her hardest to appear absorbed in the work, Elizabeth became instantly aware of the precise second that Burk pulled his gaze from her. It felt like an intense loss of pressure on her skin, as if something had suddenly blocked out the burning rays of the hot Texas sun.

Sighing with relief, Elizabeth allowed her eyes to close briefly while she tried to collect her wits. This feeling for Burk had grown so much! It astonished her how physically aware she was of him now. This situation could quickly become intolerable.

Should she quit and go back to New York? Back to her family and Trevor?

"No!"

"What was that, Elizabeth?" Burk asked.

"What?" she asked, glancing up at him guiltily. Had she said that out loud?

"You said something?" Burk's eyebrows rose as he peered back at her.

"I think . . . my pen. . . . It's running out of ink. It's my favorite one." No matter how hard she tried to hold her eyes steady, the gaze she directed at him seemed to waver anyway.

"Don't worry, Elizabeth," Burk reassured her as he turned a little more in the seat, then reached a well-muscled arm back to her. Resting a tanned hand lightly on her knee, Burk gazed deeply into her nervous eyes.

"When we get back to the dig, I'll get you another one like it. As a matter of fact, you and I should make a shopping trip into Lubbock. You probably haven't seen much of the city, and there's this bookstore near the university that I'd like to show you. I could use some drafting supplies, and I'm sure they'll have your type of pen there." He reached out and gently pulled the pen from between her slack fingers, then squinted at the brand name imprinted on it.

"Yes, I'm sure they have that type there. We'll go tomorrow. All right?" He patted her knee one more time. "You aren't still upset about what happened on the cliff, are you?"

"Of course I am," she wanted to scream at him. Seeing him dangle a finger's grip away from death. . . . But right now it seemed that his touch might be her main problem.

"It was a dangerous situation, Burk. Surely you don't

expect me to simply forget all about it.'' Her words were accusing, but her voice bordered so close to pleading.

''No, of course not,'' he answered, shifting uncomfortably under her scrutiny. ''But we're all okay now. You shouldn't be worrying about it. I understand how upset you've been by it, and I'm sorry about the stress it's caused you. Please, Elizabeth,'' his eyes pleaded with her now, ''let's try to forget it.''

She would have to put a stop to this. Ruthlessly, she cut off all thought of her feelings for Burk. Now that she recognized what was happening, and knew the danger of letting it develop any further, Elizabeth swore that she would see an end to it immediately. And she wouldn't have to go back to New York to do that, she promised herself. She could squelch every thought and fantasy of Burk the moment it entered her mind. She would avoid him, stay away as much as possible. Right now would be the end of her growing problem with Burk.

''What do you say, Elizabeth? Can we put it behind us?''

Put it behind us? He echoed her thoughts, saying just what she wanted to do. She wanted to put all those crazy feelings about Burk behind her.

''Let's forget all about that business on the edge of the cliff, and get our minds back on our work,'' he said, then smiled encouragingly at her.

The cliff? He was talking about the cliff. She had allowed her mind to go off on a tangent of its own again. Thank goodness he had no idea what she was thinking about. But maybe she was wrong to feel that there was something growing between them. Maybe the feelings were all one-sided. A grimace crept across Elizabeth's face. But that shouldn't matter now.

He wanted her to forget all about it, so she could get back to working on his book. That was all he was concerned about. That shouldn't hurt her, but it did. How very like Burk Sutherland.

Calming her nerves, Elizabeth gazed steadily back at him. "Sure, I'm ready to get back to work, if you are."

"Great," he said, with one of his dazzling smiles. "There are a few facts I'd like you to verify. The information should be here, in this book. You could work on that, while I go over my notes on the end of the Paleo-Indian period and the beginning of the Archaic period. We should be ready to put the first part of the book away in the next few days."

"All right," Elizabeth agreed as she took the book from him. "Are these the points you want verified?" she asked, pulling a paper from inside the book. It was covered with the neat lettering she had come to recognize as being the only way Burk ever wrote anything. If she had any idea how to analyze handwriting, she suspected it would show what a control-oriented person Burk could be.

Silence filled the rest of the ride, punctuated with short bursts of conversation as she and Burk exchanged information; always on the work they were doing, and always as brief as possible.

"Home sweet home," Ned's voice rang out, startling the stillness that filled the jeep for the last several miles. Ned steered the jeep onto the restricted access road that led to the archaeological dig. Elizabeth and Burk closed and repacked the various books and files scattered about the seats and floor.

"I've got the box," Burk told her. "Do you have your papers?"

"Yes." She answered, her mind swirling, as they set out for the office building.

"We could get a lot of work done in the time we have left today," Burk suggested after Ned left them at the edge of the compound clearing.

Elizabeth glanced at her watch as she paced along beside Burk. Her mind whirled furiously as she contemplated what to do.

"I know it's a little after one o'clock," Burk said as they paused in his office doorway. "Why don't we meet back here after a quick lunch?"

Now would be the perfect time, she urged herself. This would be a great opportunity to stand up to Burk, like Clare suggested she do. There was no reason to let him drive her so hard. She had been up since well before dawn, and it would be perfectly reasonable for her to expect a break, especially after the ordeal she'd been through that morning.

"I'd like a break," she began. "If you wouldn't mind." She felt proud of how strong her voice sounded. "I'm a bit tired from the drive . . . and I think I could use a nap after lunch. That is, if you don't mind?" Oh! She hadn't meant to add that.

"A nap?"

Burk sounded as if he had never heard of such a thing. Elizabeth waited, staring expectantly up at him. What would this big man make of her request? He stared back, almost as if he were afraid to say anything to her.

Finally, he managed, "I suppose that would be okay—"

"Great!" she hastily exclaimed as she dashed in and set her papers on the typing table. "I'll see you later this afternoon." She slipped by him and got out the door before he had a chance to say anything else.

Elizabeth silently congratulated herself while she grabbed a quick sandwich on the way to her room. She had done a marvelous job of standing up for her needs, and felt pleased that it turned out so well.

The room was deserted when she arrived. Clare must still be at work, or out to lunch with friends. So Elizabeth sat by the open window to eat her sandwich in happy solitude. Kicking off her shoes, she propped her tired feet up on the windowsill and rocked back in the chair.

From her vantage point, she could see the offices, the other dormitory, where Burk and Ned lived, the compound clearing and the matrix washing facility. Two students crossed the clearing carrying bags of matrix, the soil removed from the dig, that had been bagged and labeled. They must be on their way to wash it. She'd done some of the bagging for the square-unit Burk was working on now, and even washed matrix with Clare on several occasions.

It was fantastic to see all the tiny things hidden in the soil revealed when she spread it on screens and rinsed it with water. The small grains of soil drained through the mesh holes, leaving bits of pottery, small bone fragments, and shells on the wire screen.

This place . . . it made her feel alive. She curled her toes in delight. Living and working at the archaeological dig was almost everything she'd hoped for in New York. Pulling off her peach headband, Elizabeth shook back her thick, chestnut mane.

The people of Texas were really as friendly as she heard they were. And the weather was clear and sunny the whole time. Today she had seen the most breathtaking scenery. . . .

"Breathtaking," she murmured, then snorted in disgust. "Who am I trying to kid? It was almost life-taking!" A wry smile tugged at the corners of her mouth as she thought about how hard Burk tried to talk her out of being upset about that near-disaster earlier today.

His eyes had grown a pale, smoky gray as he attempted to reason with her. They were almost magical in appearance at that moment. That man seemed to be able to draw something right from her soul. A want, or a need, that she didn't even know she had.

For the rest of the summer, she would have to be extra careful around Dr. Burk Sutherland. He was turning out to be more of a hazard than she'd ever anticipated.

"You've got to be kidding!" Burk almost shouted at Ned. The two of them stood alone in Burk's office the next day. Moments earlier, Elizabeth stepped out for lunch when Ned dropped by for a chat with Burk.

"No, I'm not. It was fairly plain to see, Burk."

"Well you're way off the mark with this, buddy. I mean, the very idea is absolutely ridiculous." Burk ran his fingers through his unruly hair and paced around his small office. There wasn't much distance for his long, determined strides to cover, so he stopped at his desk to face Ned who had withdrawn to relative safety, perched on the edge of it.

"I don't think so, I think I'm more on the mark than you're willing to accept." Ned's even timbre stood in stark contrast to Burk's alarmed voice. "I'm telling you, Burk. There's something developing between you two."

Again Burk's restless fingers strafed his dark hair. Part of what Ned said was true, he reflected. Elizabeth looked exhausted from their ordeal yesterday morning, and he was still suffering pangs of guilt about how frightened she'd been.

"But Ned, that's . . . that's simply ludicrous!"

"I may have been hanging off the side of a cliff at the time, but I could still tell the difference in her voice when you dropped over the side to help me." Ned pivoted to face Burk, who was retreating to the solid support of his desk chair. "And there's no denying that it was you she hovered over when we were both lying on the ground recovering our breath."

"Well, she's my assistant," Burk declared defiantly. "It only stands to reason that she would gravitate toward me in a moment of stress."

"Yeah, right." The irony in Ned's voice rang out as sharp as the Folsom spear point lying on Burk's desk. "But if that's true, and Elizabeth has absolutely no interest in you—beyond the boss/assistant thing—then you've got a real one-sided thing going on in your head."

"What?" Burk sprang from his chair again, gaping at his friend.

"Simmer down, simmer down," Ned urged, reaching out and firmly pushing Burk back into his chair. "I can see that this comes as quite a shock to you, Dr. Sutherland. As a brilliant scientist, and trained observer, you should have noticed the signs before. But luckily I'm here to point them out to you.''

Ned drew a deep breath. ''You've got a thing for your pretty little assistant.''

''That's absurd!'' Burk thundered, half rising from his chair.

''Where have I heard that before?'' Ned asked under his breath. ''Honestly, Burk, take a look at the facts.'' Ned held up a hand and began ticking off his points on his fingers. ''You hang on her every word. You stare at her with those big puppy-dog eyes. You ogle her behind every time she takes a step away from you—''

''I don't ogle!'' Burk shook his head. ''I like her, that's all. She's a competent typist, she takes good notes, she's a hard worker, just like J—''

''Just like Jean-Paul,'' Ned interrupted.

''Yes, just like Jean-Paul,'' Burk emphatically agreed.

''And how many times did you find yourself leaning over to catch a whiff of Jean-Paul's perfume?''

''It's not her perfume,'' he protested loudly, shaking his finger at Ned. ''It's her shampoo. . . . '' Burk's voice trailed off and his mouth hung open in disbelief. He did that! He did it all the time!

That first day here in the office, when he accidentally caught the scent of fresh apricot in her hair, he'd been so tantalized. He leaned close to her the next day and found that her shining chestnut locks still smelled just as refreshing as he remembered.

Since that day, he made a habit of drawing a deep breath when their heads were close. A few times he even devised excuses to be close to Elizabeth, and once, was pleasantly surprised to discover she'd switched to an apple-scented shampoo. It reminded him of the cool, crisp apples he had as afternoon snacks when he was a child. With alarm, he remembered almost asking Elizabeth why she had changed shampoo that day. At the time, he'd stopped himself when he realized the impulse was silly.

"There it is!" Ned's triumphant tone shattered Burk's reverie.

"What? There's what?"

"That puppy-dog look you get when you're thinking about Elizabeth."

Sighing heavily, Burk leaned back in his chair. "You may be right, Ned."

"You know I'm right. And you'd better take steps to make sure your heart doesn't interfere with your head. You have too much riding on this book to let anything interfere with your work right now. Becoming involved with your assistant? That's bound to cause a lot of interference. It could also raise some eyebrows, Burk. You've got to be careful."

"Look who's giving me advice! The guy who goes out partying with his and everybody else's assistant every Saturday night. Good grief, Ned—"

"That's partying, Burk. People having fun. This thing between you and Elizabeth, it's not the same. It could cause you real trouble."

"I still think you're in just as vulnerable a position as I am, Ned. But honestly, there's really nothing to all this," Burk protested.

"Let me ask you two questions, Burk. What would happen if I didn't get my research finished?"

"Well—" Burk began.

"I'd get an extension. But what happens if you don't get yours done on time?"

"I lose Peru." Burk's face clouded.

"You have to face the facts, pal."

"I never thought of it like that, Ned. It almost makes me wish Jean-Paul would come back." He rubbed his chin thoughtfully. "Almost."

Chapter Five

Seated at his desk, Burk smiled up at her as he carefully laid the last sheet of paper in a white cardboard box. "The first half of the book is finished. We've actually done it, Elizabeth. We've caught up with my schedule." A sparkle of delight flashed in his smoky eyes, filling her with a sense of warmth.

The long, hard hours of work had paid off, and Burk looked as if the weight of the world were finally off his shoulders. Elizabeth smiled back at him, feeling the tension ease from her body as well. She wanted so much to help Burk reach his goal, and now they were halfway there. It gave her a sense of accomplishment that she'd never known before.

"So, the Paleo-Indian period and all its spear hunters are behind us." She beamed as she straightened up. "We've covered from 11,500 to 8,500 B.C. Let's get started on the Archaic Period. We've got half a day left, and no reason to waste it."

Chuckling, Burk rose from his chair. "Hold on. I disagree." He took her by the shoulders and steered her out the office door.

"Burk—" she protested lightly, while trying to latch her fingers over the door post.

"I think we have an excellent reason to waste the rest of this day." He uncurled her fingers and, after locking the office door, pulled her across the nearly deserted compound. As she continued to sputter objections, Burk paused long enough to hold a hushing finger across her lips. "We haven't been away from this place since our little excursion to Mulberry canyon almost two weeks ago. We've done a fantastic job, and we both deserve a break."

The firm gentleness of his finger brushing intimately against her lips brought Elizabeth's protests to a sputtering halt. Then Burk's eyes widened in astonishment, almost as if he were surprised at his own actions. With a quick jerk, he pulled his hand away from her face, and took a small step back.

"We need some time away from here. We need to rejuvenate ourselves before we tackle the last half of the book," he explained.

"I see. But what do you have in mind? Something relaxing?"

"Not exactly," he replied mischievously. His left brow crept upward as he took her hand and urged her on toward the parking area.

"What do you mean by that? Where are we going?" she asked, but Burk never bothered to answer. He didn't even slow his pace.

"At least tell me if I'm dressed all right for wherever you're taking me."

That request finally got his attention. Burk glanced down at her as he tugged her along close at his side. He eyed her shining chestnut hair that she'd swept back from her face and secured by one of the tortoiseshell headbands she wore so often.

She had dressed casually, as always, for a day spent at the dig and puttering around the office. A canary yellow cotton blouse and blue jeans made no fashion statement, but Elizabeth enjoyed the comfortable feel of the outfit. Her one concession to coordinating her clothing was her bright yellow tennis shoes. Burk's eyes seemed to linger on them longer than was necessary, causing her a slight buzz of embarrassment.

"Do you own any western boots?"

"Western boots?" she asked, staring at him in bewilderment.

"Cowboy boots," he elaborated. "You know, with heels and pointed toes?"

Cowboy boots? She did think fleetingly about buying a pair for her trip while she was still in New York, but never found the time to do anything more than think about it. Then, once here, she was glad she hadn't. Since she spent all her time at the dig, she would never have a chance to wear them. Most of the researchers either wore tennis shoes or work boots.

"No," she said shaking her head. "I don't have any."

"Then you're dressed fine," he declared as he continued to lead her to the jeep. "Hop in, we're wasting daylight."

Elizabeth did as she was told, taking Burk's offered hand

to steady herself as she stepped up into the vehicle. The jeep wasn't very high off the ground, and she probably didn't really need the support, but there was no reason to avoid touching Burk. She had her feelings for him firmly under control.

But there it was, that electric sensation, that quiet thrill. It happened every time his leg brushed up against hers in the office, or their hands touched as they worked side by side at the dig. The sensation was immediately followed by a flurry of confusion as she fought to damp down her emotions.

Burk Sutherland evoked such a strong response in her, and Elizabeth knew that she was playing with fire, allowing things to continue as they were. She had to face the fact. When it came to Burk, she wasn't in control of anything.

It would be so easy to give in to the temptation to reach out and press her lips to his. Sometimes, late at night when they were working alone, Elizabeth felt a tugging desire to lean closer to him, to run her hand up his arm, to feel the strong muscles of his jaw against her palm.

The driver's door clanged shut as Burk joined her in the jeep, and she glanced guiltily at his seductive profile. He directed his piercing gaze through the windshield as he steered the jeep from the bumpy service road onto the highway, but she could still sense his intensity.

The profile of that strong jaw, that she was so familiar with, jutted out firmly. At the base of his corded neck she saw the pulsing of his blood as it raced through the faint blue line of a vein that ran close to the surface of his sun-bronzed flesh.

Wherever they were going, whatever they were going to

do, she didn't doubt that he would be dressed just right for it. His pale gold chamois shirt, with the sleeves rolled halfway up his tanned forearms, and his faded, well-worn jeans, suited his frame and his personality perfectly. As usual, he had on his scuffed, tan boots, their thick, notched soles adding an inch or more to his lanky six feet. Burk looked like he would be comfortable, and in command, no matter where he was.

Steeling herself against the prodding hunger she felt for Burk, Elizabeth fixed her gaze out the windshield, just as his was.

"I thought you might like to have a real western experience while you're here in Texas."

A distinct note of glee echoed in his voice, giving Elizabeth a wary feeling. "What exactly do you mean by a western experience?" she asked.

"Ever been on a horse?"

She glanced sideways in utter amazement, too stunned to answer.

A lopsided grin spread across Burk's face as he arched his brows. "I take it that's a 'no'?"

"Y—Yes," she stammered. "I mean, no, I've never been on a horse." Then the excitement bubbled out of her as she barraged him with questions. "Is that what we're going to do? Are we going to ride horses? With real western saddles?"

"Yep!" He managed to squeeze an answer in among her questions.

"Where? Are we near the stables?"

"Yes. In fact, we're almost there. I have a friend who

lives out on the edge of Ransom Canyon, and he has a couple of mares he lets me borrow now and then.''

"On the edge of a canyon?'' Her eyes were instantly wide with fright.

"I don't mean that literally,'' Burk quickly assured her, patting her arm to calm her fears.

A tingling sense of confusion swept over her as his broad hand lingered on her arm. Her thoughts and senses focused on the feel of his touch, as everything else faded away. His contact grew bolder as his thumb traced lazy circles on her bare skin. Afraid to move and lose his touch, Elizabeth held herself still and endured the near torture of Burk's light caress.

Could she reach up with her other hand and cover his? But that might lead Burk to believe that she wanted something more. He was only trying to comfort her, she reminded herself, and her silly feelings were putting too much into a casual touch.

The very idea that he might have some sort of feeling for her, other than a pure professional one, was sheer fantasy. This nonsense had better stop, she scolded herself.

"His ranch is near a canyon, a gently sloping canyon,'' he emphasized. "And we'll be riding on a nice, flat plateau. Land that looks exactly like this,'' he said as he took his hand away to gesture at the countryside they were driving through.

Elizabeth couldn't resist the impulse that swept over her. She clamped a hand over the warm spot on her arm where Burk had rubbed tingling circles into her skin. With an effort, she managed to get her breathing under control before her deep breaths became obvious, then smiled with feigned confidence.

"It'll be perfectly safe. Trust me."

Burk smiled at her and Elizabeth would have sworn she saw a twinkle in his eye.

The barns, tall red structures amid pastures of deep grass, came in sight first. Cows dotted the green expanses, with their heads down, slowly munching their way across the landscape. Three horses stood in a small paddock near one of the barns. As they drew closer, Elizabeth saw a lean man emerge from the white clapboard house set a few yards from the cluster of barns. He waved a friendly greeting to them as they stepped from the jeep.

Burk enthusiastically shook hands with the man as he introduced Elizabeth to the owner of the horses. "My old friend, Jess," Burk said. "We went to college together."

"That's right," the man said with a slow drawl. He had that distinct Texas way of stretching out words that Elizabeth had come to recognize very soon after her arrival here. "Got your horses saddled up and waiting, Burk."

Surprise flashed across Elizabeth's face. Burk must have called his friend before leaving the Lubbock Lake dig, although she couldn't remember him doing so. Perhaps he made the call when she stepped out of the office for more coffee. Still, at the time it had seemed to her that Burk's idea to take her horseback riding was purely spontaneous. But he obviously planned it way before suggesting it to her.

In an odd way, Elizabeth felt disappointed as she thought about it. Somehow, she'd gotten the idea that Burk felt a

strong impulse to be with her that he just dropped everything and ran off with her.

"You didn't need to use up your valuable time saddling
the horses, Jess. I could have done that," Burk told his
friend as he led them to the paddock.

As she followed a few steps behind the men, it occurred
to Elizabeth that there could be another way to interpret
this. Since it was obviously something he planned, then that
meant he'd been thinking about ways to spend time with
her away from work. That meant she *was* on his mind.
Could he have the same feelings for her as she had for
him?

Jess held the bay mare steady as Burk helped Elizabeth
into the saddle. She adjusted her feet in the roomy stirrups
and straightened up. Wow! This was a long way from the
ground. From up on the horse's back, she could see for
miles. What an incredible perspective.

"What's my horse's name?"

"That's Nelly," Jess replied. "This one here's Nessy,"
he said, indicating the horse whose reins he held for Burk.

"Now just hold tight to that." Burk indicated the large
saddle horn in front of Elizabeth.

"How convenient to have a handle on the front of the
saddle," Elizabeth exclaimed with delight as she gripped
the round piece of leather.

Burk swung up into the saddle of the roan mare beside
Elizabeth's bay. "It's not exactly a handle. It's a saddle
horn. When a cowboy ropes an animal, he ties the end of
the rope around the saddle horn."

"I see." Elizabeth took the information he offered without batting an eyelash. Burk taught her many things about

the working routine of an archaeologist since her arrival here in Texas, and never, since that fateful discussion about awls, had he made her feel the least bit foolish about her questions or comments. A secret smile spread across her face as she watched Burk settle his athletic build into Nessy's saddle.

"Now you let her have her head, and she'll follow ole Nessy there," Jess told Elizabeth, indicating the horse Burk sat astride. "Leave the reins looped over the saddle horn, just like they are, unless you want to stop." He picked up the joined, leather strips. "Then, you gently pull back on 'em. Nelly'll stop for you."

"Thanks, Jess." Burk waved to his friend, then swatted Elizabeth's horse on the rump, sending it slowly trotting away from the stable.

Luckily her fingers were laced around the big saddle horn in a death grip. Elizabeth felt herself jerk backward and she felt that a tight hold was all that kept her from tumbling off the horse's back end. Burk caught up with her before she reached the open gate, and Nessy's presence seemed to cause Nelly to slow down. Soon, they were ambling slowly side by side across the open prairie.

"You should have warned me back at the stable," she chided Burk.

"Good!" he encouraged her as he grinned broadly. "You're loose enough to talk finally."

"Oh, I don't look all that bad. Do I?"

"Not to me."

His words sent her heart racing, and her mind following it, down paths of past daydreams. But, she pulled her thoughts to an abrupt stop, his remark couldn't be anything other than a casual observation. Could it?

"You look like you're having a good time," Burk said.

Elizabeth tried to relax. When they left Burk's office, she'd had such high hopes for a tranquil afternoon, full of easy conversation and fun. They both needed time away from the stress of their demanding work. But this undercurrent of tension that she felt, it seemed to keep popping up.

"What'll I do if we need to turn?" she asked, determined to get her mind moving away from those disturbing thoughts of Burk.

"Don't worry about that right now. Your horse will stay with mine. We'll ride out to a trail that runs beside that fence there, and I'll give you a riding lesson," he said as he pointed ahead.

"Promise?"

"I promise." His smile broadened at her eagerness.

"All right," Elizabeth agreed as she hung on to the saddle horn. "Your friend has a beautiful place here."

"Yes. Jess is really a lucky man. He got this place from his uncle, and hasn't regretted it a day since. It must be great to have a place to belong to, to always come home to."

Elizabeth recognized a wistful tone in Burk's voice. "I don't know. It might be more fun to live in lots of different places, to move around and see the world."

"Is that why you came out here? To see the world?"

She smiled at him. "I suppose so, to some degree. But more than anything, I wanted to get involved in something worth doing for once in my life. I wanted to feel necessary."

"You're very necessary to me," he said as he eyed her evenly.

"Thanks, really," she replied, then smiled. "But I didn't say that just to get a compliment."

"That was simply the truth. But what about seeing the world? You must get to take a lot of trips, don't you?"

Listening to the clopping of the horse's hooves on the packed soil of the trail, Elizabeth thought about Burk's question. Yes, she did travel a bit, but it always felt like more of a temporary reprieve from a prison sentence than a vacation. She always had to go back home.

"I do take a trip occasionally. And what about you?" she asked, steering the conversation away from herself. "What brought you to Texas?"

"A grant," he replied.

Elizabeth chuckled softly. How very like Burk to take her literally. "I meant, what made you want to get away from your home . . . to come here."

"Oh." He had the decency to look chagrined as he acknowledged her amusement. "I've always been interested in this region, and the spear hunters of the Paleo-Indian Period. An article I wrote for the Archaeological Institute's magazine, *American Journal*, led to a grant for my book. It really wasn't a matter of my leaving home, it's just that my work took me away a long time ago."

"How long ago?" she asked.

He shrugged. "Shortly after college, I suppose."

"And you're happy doing what you're doing?"

"I love my work," he answered honestly. "It may not show, but I enjoy writing."

She smiled wryly at him, and felt happy when he returned the smile. "Have you had much experience writing?"

"Not a lot. I've had three articles in *American Journal*, and a few in *Archaeology*. Ned and I coauthored one while we were in college together."

"Have you known Ned long?"

"We met in college. I hadn't seen him since graduation, until I came here to Texas."

"It's a small world," she said, then laughed at the cliché.

Burk grinned openly at her, sharing in the humor she found in the moment.

When she managed to recover her composure, she asked, "Would you have copies of your articles back in your office? I'd like to read them."

"Do I ever!" He rolled his eyes. "Laminated, photocopied, and filed. Without those, I wouldn't be where I am right now."

"I think Nelly there has something to do with that." Elizabeth pointed at Burk's horse.

Laughter bubbled up between them, thrilling Elizabeth. He had the good manners to laugh at her jokes, no matter how feeble they were. Something else to admire about Burk Sutherland, she mused. If she wasn't careful, she might find out that Burk was the most perfect man in the world— something she had long suspected, she realized.

"But it's true. I do have copies and I'd be delighted to show them to you."

"And is it true that you wouldn't be here without having been published?"

"Absolutely! Publishing is everything, if you hope to get the big grants and the big jobs. That's why this book means so much to me."

"Are you hoping for another grant?" A flicker of apprehension accompanied her words, and rippled through her. Would another grant take him away from Texas? But what a silly fear that was. It didn't matter whether Burk would be leaving or not. Soon she would be the one leaving. She would be going back to New York and the life that waited for her there.

Her family, her fiancé, and her volunteer work at the museum. That would be her future. While Burk's future probably lay in some remote corner of the world, far from New York, far from her.

Burk must have seen the pain on her features, and misinterpreted it as physical discomfort. Reaching over to Nelly's reins, he pulled the horse to a stop beside his.

"Would you like to get down and stretch your leg muscles?"

"That might be a good idea," she agreed, willing a smile onto her lips.

Burk quickly dismounted and draped his horse's reins onto the ground. Seeing her worried expression, he answered her unspoken question. "Nelly's trained to ground-tie. She won't wander more than a few steps when the end of her reins are on the ground. Your horse Nessy, is trained to do the same thing."

His strong hands almost completely encircled her waist as he lifted her from the saddle and lowered her till her feet gently touched the ground. Elizabeth felt her knees buckle and clutched at Burk's arms, only to be enfolded in his warm embrace.

Her mind reeled as her betraying heart raced.

"Are you all right?" he asked, while steadying her.

His warm breath brushed across her upturned cheek, and Elizabeth felt her resolve melting. Now would be the time to take a step back from his solid body. There was no time to waste, but she couldn't get her brain to command her legs to work. She looked up into Burk's smoldering gray eyes.

"I . . . I'm fine."

"I guess the question should have been, are your legs all right?" He kept his arms banded around Elizabeth's slender waist.

Being in his arms felt so satisfying, so right. Her body molded itself to his, and the fit was perfect. Burk's chest seemed to rise and fall faster now that she was against it and able to feel its every movement.

"Elizabeth?"

She gazed up at him, her eyes drifting down his ruggedly handsome features, from his strong brow to his full lips. Her lips felt flushed and hot. What would it feel like if she pulled his head down to hers? Joined her lips to his?

"Elizabeth, would you like to sit down for a moment?"

His words finally penetrated her desire-fogged mind. Shaking her head, she managed to take that step back from him, although it was a very small step. But it managed to break most of the physical contact between them that had stunned her so much.

Burk cleared his throat and shifted from one foot to the

other, his eyes shifting from bushes to rocks to clouds, anywhere but in her direction.

As she slid her arms from his, Burk raised his broad hands and raked splayed fingers through his tangled hair. Clearing his throat again, he asked, "Do you need a rest? It can be a strain on your legs, riding a horse for the first time."

Something inside her heart told her that Burk was sparing her feelings. All the horses had done was plod slowly along since leaving Jess's place. There should be no reason for her to be so affected by the short ride. He must have sensed her feelings for him, the feelings she had been fighting for so long.

"I'm fine," she lied. "I just felt a little woozy for a moment."

"Well, let's sit here for a minute or so," Burk indicated a small outcropping of rock a few feet away from the trail they'd been following. "We came out here to enjoy the scenery, so we ought to take the time to do that."

Elizabeth followed Burk to the rock and perched beside him, stretching out her long legs. They did feel a bit tight, she realized. Sitting in the saddle was definitely hard on certain parts of a person's anatomy, she decided as she rubbed her aching thighs. Maybe Burk hadn't noticed her strong reaction to his touch. Maybe . . .

Burk's soft chuckle brought her head up and she looked around to see what he was laughing at.

"City girls," he snorted in mock disgust.

"Look who's talking. Philadelphia isn't exactly the Wild West, you know," she retorted. A twinkle in his eye warned Elizabeth that Burk wasn't through teasing her yet.

"Ah, but it's eons closer than Manhattan, my dear. And my folks live in a suburb, one that allows horses."

"I surrender," Elizabeth held her hands up. He called her "dear"! Perhaps it was only a casual reference, spoken more in jest than anything else, but it still sent her blood singing through her veins.

Elizabeth reveled in her secret desire for Burk Sutherland. She had been in his arms, felt his moist, sweet breath on her cheek, and heard him call her "dear." This was turning out to be the most exciting day she'd spent here in Texas. But, she cautioned herself, it's only a secret fantasy. Nothing could ever come of her yearnings for Burk. Nothing must ever come of this need she felt.

Burk was not her future. Trevor was.

"Honestly, Elizabeth, you're doing fine, just fine."

"Then how about that riding lesson you promised me?"

"I did promise, didn't I? And I always keep my promises, Elizabeth, always." His eyes seemed to burn into her.

Her heart raced as Burk helped her mount. Then he kept his hands over hers while instructing her on the proper way to hold the reins. The two pieces of leather were knotted together at the saddle horn.

"Hold the knot in one hand." He curled her fingers around it. "That's right. Now the excess length of rein; lay that across your leg." Burk allowed her to keep her other hand firmly clenched around the saddle horn. "After a little more time in the saddle, you won't need that safety hold."

Under Burk's gentle instruction, Elizabeth had Nelly turning left and right, and stopping with controlled movements of the reins she held low and loose.

"I think we're ready to start back, don't you?" Burk

asked as he gave her an encouraging smile. "We can take the same trail that runs beside the fence there, it'll take us back. You take the lead this time, you're ready for it."

"Oh no. I don't think—"

"You can do it," Burk encouraged her.

"But what if Nelly decides to run off and I can't stop her?"

"Nelly would never run off and leave Nessy. I swear," he promised solemnly, holding up a hand as if he were in court.

Resigned to doing as Burk asked, Elizabeth managed to turn Nelly back toward her home. A flush of pride spread through her as she realized she was in control of their destination now.

"This is great," she exclaimed, sending a smile over her shoulder at Burk. "She'll do anything I tell her to do."

"You're a good rider, Elizabeth."

Looking back again, Elizabeth searched his face for any sign of teasing. There certainly hadn't been any in his tone of voice. Just then Nelly lurched sideways with a quick, hard jolt, and took a couple of small steps to recover her balance. Elizabeth dropped the reins and grabbed onto the saddle horn with both hands. Nelly resumed plodding along, without Elizabeth's hand to guide her, following the well-worn path beside the fence.

"Let's stop a minute," Burk called.

Taking a steadying breath, Elizabeth forced herself to let go of the saddle horn long enough to grasp the reins that were resting on the horse's neck. Remembering her instructions, she pulled gently but firmly back on the reins until Nelly stopped, then she released the pressure.

Burk brought Nessy up beside her and dismounted in one swift movement. "Let me help you down. I'd like to take a look at Nelly's foot."

"Why? What's wrong?"

"I don't know. Probably nothing," he assured her as he shrugged. "But she's been favoring her right front leg since she did that little jig back there," he indicated the trail behind them with his thumb.

This time, with her attention focused on the horse, Elizabeth wasn't as overwhelmed by his touch. She stood at Nessy's head, holding the reins as Burk instructed her to do. As Burk raised the animal's leg, Elizabeth tried to peer over his shoulder.

"What is it? Have I done something to her?" Nelly snorted through big nostrils and the blast of warm air ticked the hairs on Elizabeth's arm.

"That's Nelly laughing at you, not me," Burk said, as he put the animal's foot down. "You didn't do anything. She just had a stone lodged in her frog." He held up a small, white pebble.

"Her frog?" Elizabeth asked, disbelief written all over her features. "Is that some kind of a joke?"

"No." Burk motioned for her to come around to Nelly's side as he lifted the foot again. "This V-shaped section here in the middle of a horse's foot is called the frog. It can be painful if a horse gets a stone embedded in these grooves here," he indicated the area where he had removed the offending stone. Setting the horse's foot down one more time, he gave the animal a pat on the neck. "She should be fine, but I think we should let her walk back without a rider.''

''Oh. But how will I get back?'' Elizabeth's eyes widened.

''You'll ride with me,'' he replied simply. ''Nessy can carry both of us back with no problem. Unless you were planning on doing some galloping on the way back.'' Burk raised an eyebrow teasingly at her.

''No,'' Elizabeth vehemently denied, unsure if she was denying the desire to gallop, or the desire to be so close to Burk.

''Good,'' he said, nodding firmly. ''Nelly will follow us at her own pace. All I need to do is loop the reins over her saddle horn. Do you need help mounting Nessy?''

''I can manage,'' Elizabeth quickly replied as she used all her strength to pull herself up into the saddle. Nessy was even taller than Nelly, and the height was almost frightening. To make matters worse, the stirrups were longer, so much so that her toes barely touched them. She sat in the roomy saddle, her back ramrod straight, staring down at Burk who stood at her knee as if he was waiting for something.

''Elizabeth,'' he said, placing one hand on the saddle, inches away from her knee.

''Yes?'' She tried not to sound breathless, as that intense awareness of him swept over her again.

''The stirrup. I need it for a minute.''

Her cheeks flamed red. ''Oh, of course,'' she said as she pulled her left foot from the stirrup to allow Burk to mount.

"And you might want to lean forward, so I don't squash you," he added.

Despite the saddle horn, she did her best to flatten herself against Nessy's neck. The musty scent of hay and dust rose from the animal's coat and tickled Elizabeth's nose. She fought hard to keep the sneeze that built up in her from bursting forth. But it became so hard to concentrate on that as she felt the saddle lurch sideways. Burk's body settled behind her, on the end of the colorful, woven saddle blanket.

"You can sit up now." He almost chuckled as he spoke.

With the need to hold herself out of Burk's way gone, Elizabeth felt the need to end the tickling in her nose grow. Just as she got her body straight in the saddle, her head snapped forward and she sneezed. Burk's arms flew around to steady her as she grabbed handfuls of mane for support.

Fighting hard to get breath to go back in her body, she felt too conscious of Burk's arms holding her tight. She fought the urge to gulp air, but was painfully aware of her ribs expanding, of Burk's skin sliding across hers as she moved. Elizabeth tried to fight the urge to lean back into his embrace, to caress his powerful arms.

"I'm . . . fine now," she managed to mumble. "Thanks."

Slowly, Burk relinquished his firm grip on her. His hands slid over her arms, his fingers trailing down her sides.

"Are you ready to go?" he asked softly.

Only inches separated his lips from her ear. She felt his words as much as she heard them.

"Yes," she answered meekly, hoping that her breath wasn't as ragged as his sounded. This was definitely going to be a long ride, a very long ride.

Chapter Six

The horse plodded along as Elizabeth concentrated on the vast landscape surrounding them. There must be something around here to take her mind off the sensation of Burk's broad chest brushing up against her back. But it was just her luck that they were in the middle of a flat, open range. A few short mesquite trees dotted the horizon to the west. There was nothing else in sight but the fence they followed and clumps of wild prairie grass for miles around.

The vast sky stretched overhead, the same sky she told Clare she could stare at for hours and hours. But right now, Elizabeth would have given anything to have something, anything, pop up for them to talk about.

Burk cleared his throat, and, with his right arm that was stretched around her, shifted his grip on the reins, accidentally brushing her thigh. "I was telling you about what I hope will happen when my book is published," he said.

"Yes!" She enthusiastically latched onto the subject. Talking about his work would keep her mind off what she felt through her thin blouse. Absently, she rubbed her right thigh while mentally urging him to continue.

"I'm hoping for a directorship of a dig in Peru."

"Peru?" She felt a wave of distress threaten to overcome her. "But that's so far away."

"It's not as far as you think," he argued as he tugged Nessy's reins to steer her wider around a large paddle cactus that grew near the trail.

Elizabeth stared down at the green plant with its countless thorns as Nessy skirted it. The purple balls of fruit budding from the edges of the round paddles looked incongruous on such a hazardous plant.

"When would you be going?"

"I hope around Christmastime. That is, if I get the job. Nothing's positive yet."

"But you'll get the position." She tried looking over her left shoulder at him as she spoke. It seemed important that he see the earnestness in her eyes. Maybe then she could believe it herself—that she was supportive of his leaving. "I have no doubt." But in that position, her face, her lips, were uncomfortably close to his, and she found her voice trailing off.

"Does it bother you to think about my going away, Elizabeth?"

A peculiar quiver started deep in her stomach as she stared into his eyes. Yes, he was right. The thought of him leaving, going so far away from her, sent shafts of apprehension spearing through her. Could that thought be causing her stomach to quiver, or could it be the closeness of his masculine form that made her feel so unsettled?

On a deeper level of her mind, she recognized how absurd it was to experience these feelings. She had no right to feel this way about Burk. Soon, she would be the one leaving. She was engaged to another man. A man who loved her, who was to be her future.

"I . . . " Her mouth hung open, as she stared, mesmerized by his smoldering gaze.

Burk slid his left hand up her arm, drawing her closer into an embrace.

Could this be real? She held her body completely motionless as his head angled down to hers, his lips reaching hers. They touched, velvet soft, and whisper quiet at first. Then Burk deepened the kiss, pressing his lips to hers, wrapping her closer in his strong embrace.

Elizabeth sank into his arms, letting him take possession of her eager mouth. His passion ignited the fervent desire that burned in her heart, and heated her body. Her muscles came to life again as she followed him down a path she wanted so desperately to explore, and he took her with him as his kiss touched her soul.

Twisting around further in the saddle, her hands came up to clutch at him, her fingers twining in the crisp fabric of his shirt, his chest heaving with each breath against the tender flesh of her palm. Elizabeth felt thrilled to realize that Burk was as deeply affected by their kiss as she was.

She allowed her left hand to roam upward, toward that wild thatch of hair she watched Burk tug at so frequently when he grew frustrated or impatient.

"Mmmm," his lips vibrated against hers. "Elizabeth,"

he managed to murmur between the tiny partings of their lips that Nessy's plodding gait caused.

She longed to tell him to stop the horse, to let them dismount. Then she could put her arms around his neck, she could pull him closer.

Suddenly, Nessy's gait changed. Elizabeth felt herself swaying as a briskness quickened the gentle rocking motion into jarring movements. Instantly Burk's head whipped up, away from hers, leaving her mind spinning in the void his absence created.

"We're almost back at Jess's place," Burk said with obvious regret. "Nessy knows she's almost home."

"Almost there already?" Elizabeth twisted back around in the saddle and stared at the unwelcome sight of the red barns looming very close. Nelly, who had been following steadily behind, must have also caught sight of home, and began trying to overtake Nessy.

"This could turn into a little race," Burk observed wryly as he reached for the reins that had slipped unnoticed from his hands some time ago. "I'd better remind Nessy that she's not the one in charge," he said as he took up a little of the slack in the leather strips.

Having no rider to control her, Nelly began trotting slowly toward home, her foot giving her no problem at all.

"Burk," Elizabeth's voice rose in alarm. "Won't she get hurt running like that?"

"Not at all. She wouldn't go faster than a walk if she was in any pain. Also, there's nothing between here and her barn that could cause her any kind of a problem."

"But she's loose. She could wander off, or get lost."

"She and Nessy roam around here all the time. They

A Find for All Time

wouldn't wander far from the barn. They know where their food is.'' Burk caressed her arm briefly as he spoke.

There was nothing else for her to object to. They would be back in a matter of minutes, their ride over, their time here almost at an end.

Elizabeth turned slightly, trying to peer back at Burk from the corner of her eye. She caught a glimpse of his profile, and saw the brooding set of his chin. It was almost the same foreboding look he had worn on that first, near-disastrous day of her arrival.

What could be causing those deep creases on his brow? Did he regret their kiss? Their dizzying, scintillating kiss. Elizabeth could think of it in no other terms.

She turned her gaze back to the buildings they were approaching. Nelly grazed under the shade of an apple tree near the white, clapboard house. The horse seemed content to munch on the dark, green grass. Jess caught sight of them as he came out of a small shed nearby, and waved hello.

Elizabeth raised her hand in a lackluster wave back to him, trying to put a brave smile on her face. But the heavy silence emanating from Burk drained her of the ability to smile genuinely. She couldn't manage to muster up a decent smile for Jess, and she was terrified he might ask her what was wrong.

As Burk brought Nessy to a halt, Jess came over to Elizabeth, and helped her dismount. ''Did you have trouble controlling Nelly?'' he asked, surprise widening his eyes.

''No,'' she quickly reassured him. ''Nelly wasn't a bit of a problem. But I let her step on a stone, Jess. I let her get hurt,'' she lamented.

"A stone?"

Jess's eyes grew wider as he absorbed her words. He struggled to keep his face straight, but Elizabeth saw the merriment dancing in his eyes.

"The poor horse!" Jess exclaimed, as he walked over to Nelly and patted her dark nose. "Maybe I should call the vet. What do you think, Burk?"

"Ah, cut it out, Jess. Can't you see you're scaring Elizabeth?" He swung down from the saddle, and planted his fists on his hips. "The horse is just fine, and you should tell her so."

The tension built in her till she felt she had to get away, or scream. "Jess," Elizabeth interrupted them before either had a chance to say anything further. "May I use your bathroom?"

"Certainly." His demeanor changed instantly. "Right through the back door there." He pointed to the house behind him. "Through the kitchen, then first door on your left."

"Thanks." Flashing him a grateful smile, she hurried inside, but still managed to overhear Jess as the screen door closed behind her.

"And there was nothing for you to do but take the little lady up on Nelly with you, so poor Nessy wouldn't get a sore tootsie. You're so noble, Burk." Jess was fighting his need to laugh so hard that the last words came out accompanied by snorts.

"Jess!" Burk hissed his friend's name.

Elizabeth hurried through the kitchen, afraid to hear anything else from the two men. The mirror in the bathroom shot her reflection back in stark relief, and she stared at herself, stunned at the deep crimson of her cheeks.

How could she have allowed herself to get so carried away by the passion she felt for Burk? The feelings she'd been denying, they fought so hard for release, and to her utter dismay, finally won.

It really happened. She kissed him! The realization sank into her mind. She had felt his arms around her, had pressed her lips to his. And his touch took her breath away. There could be no denying the wonderful sensation that astounding kiss filled her with. His body felt so solid and unyielding to her touch; his kiss, so deep and exciting.

All the nights she spent lying awake in her bed, imagining what it would be like to kiss Burk Sutherland came flooding into her mind. And now she knew. It was just as earth-shattering as she imagined it would be.

But how would things be between them right now if they hadn't arrived at the ranch at that moment? If they'd been a little farther away when they'd kissed . . .

No! She silently lamented. How could she have caused this to happen? Things between them would never be the same. There would be a new tension that would always be there now, coming between them no matter what they were doing.

Every time Burk looked at her she would wonder if he resented her kissing him.

This kiss would be haunting her mind, she knew. And there was something she would have to try to ignore, this tugging in her heart every time she came near Burk. Because the feelings she had for him could never be allowed to take control of her actions again.

There could never be anything between Burk and her. She was an engaged woman, promised to Trevor Davis. Burk had no place in her future, even if he wanted it. And he obviously didn't. That was plain to see from the way he reacted to Jess's teasing.

Turning on the faucet, Elizabeth splashed cold water on her face. Somehow, she had to work up the courage to endure the ride back to the dig with Burk.

As they left Jess's ranch just before dark, Burk felt a muscle in his jaw twitch while he fought to keep his teeth from grinding together. The only way he allowed his body to react to the tension was by letting his fingers tighten around the jeep's steering wheel. He was all too aware of the sun illuminating Elizabeth's beautiful profile as she sat mutely beside him, staring out the window at the brilliant reds and golds of the low bands of clouds.

Why? Why had he done it? Kissing her like that, on horseback of all places, and with no warning? What a terrible mistake.

She hadn't spoken two words to him since. Furtively, he stole another glance at Elizabeth, and felt his heart sink as he realized her posture looked even more stiff than before she got in the jeep.

If he could just go back in time, to right before his gaze drifted down to her luscious, full lips. If he could have resisted the urge to wrap his arm around her, to pull her closer to him . . .

But that wasn't the start of it. No. The first mistake he made was riding double with her. That was what caused the terrible wariness he sensed in her from the moment their lips parted. She must have thought he planned it all along, to get her in his arms. Then Jess made matters so much worse with his teasing.

Why hadn't he listened to Ned? Why couldn't he have controlled his desire for her until their working relationship was over? Then he could have planned things right. He could have asked Elizabeth out on a date, like normal people go on. Then she would be prepared when he showed her how he felt about her. She would have had a chance to see him in a different way. Not only as someone she worked for, not only as someone who ordered her about all day.

Things were really a mess now! Burk tightened his fingers around the steering wheel again. But this time he wouldn't speed. This seemed so much like the last time he sat behind a wheel and was mad at the world. With a jolt of surprise, he realized that was the day he learned Elizabeth would be his new assistant. He'd been so opposed to her coming that he'd taken his frustration out behind the wheel of the jeep, much to Ned's discomfort.

That behavior had been so absurd. Her coming to work at the dig was the best thing that could have happened to him.

Burk glanced briefly at her again. "Elizabeth . . . " His voice fell silent. What could he say to her? How could he tell her he was sorry without making matters worse than they already were? "I'm grateful for all the long hours you've put in lately. It feels wonderful to have my book back on track."

Geeze! That wasn't what he wanted to say. A war waged on inside him. His head wanted to tell her not to worry, that everything would be all right for her from now on. His heart wanted to tell her how much he desired her.

"Thanks. I'm glad we've made such good progress, Burk."

But they hadn't made progress personally, he lamented. "Yes. Things are going well at the dig." There had to be something he could do, there had to be a way to make things go well between them personally. He had to get their relationship back on an even keel. He had to.

"I'm going to call my fiancé today."

"Your fiancé?" Clare stopped her sporadic darting about the dorm room, and gaped at her roommate.

"Yes." Elizabeth tried hard to sound as if the idea were a spontaneous one. Each week since her arrival here in Texas she sent Trevor a letter, but this would be her first time to call him.

"I didn't know you were engaged. Is he the chap you get those packages from?"

"Yes. His name's Trevor Davis," Elizabeth answered, eyeing a small, brown box sitting on her nightstand. It was the latest package from him, still unopened. They were all the same. Probably something from Saks, picked out by Trevor's secretary, mailed by his secretary, on a schedule set up by him soon after she left. A package arrived often enough to keep her aware of him, but not often enough to make her think he felt insecure about her absence.

Elizabeth turned her back on the package, and continued to brush her hair.

"How awfully nice to have someone like that who cares

about you. No wonder you weren't starry-eyed over Burk.''

Clare's voice chattered on as she continued to dress, but Elizabeth's attention drifted down to the note lying on the dresser. Burk left it on her door sometime late last night. It told her to meet him in his office, instead of at the dig as usual.

After the tense ride back from Jess's ranch last night, Elizabeth lay awake for hours, racking her brain, trying to think of some way to create distance between them, without causing any more problems. Then it occurred to her, Burk didn't know she was engaged. No one here knew. She'd left her diamond engagement ring back home, telling herself at the time that she didn't want to risk losing it.

All she needed to do was inform Burk of her engagement to Trevor. Then it wouldn't matter that he regretted kissing her. He would know she was involved with someone else. There wouldn't be any more strained silence between them. And he would never know how much she ached to feel his arms around her once more.

Oh! That thought startled her. Could that be the real reason she was so upset? Was she afraid for Burk to know how much his touch really affected her? But that shouldn't matter to her. She was engaged to Trevor, he was her future, she reminded herself. She seemed to be reminding herself of that a lot lately.

''I thought I'd run over to the office and give Trevor a call before getting started with the day's work.'' And be certain to be on the phone with him when Burk arrives.

''Why haven't you told me about this fiancé before?''

''The subject never came up.''

"But when I asked you about those packages . . . "

Elizabeth was at a loss. Why hadn't she told Clare about Trevor? Wouldn't it be perfectly normal to talk about something as important as being engaged? Maybe not. Not if the engagement were something that had no real meaning for her, she realized.

But now wasn't the time to try and analyze her feelings for Trevor. This morning she had a job to do. It was imperative that she create some distance between herself and the inimitable Dr. Burk Sutherland.

"I guess I'm just shy about him, that's all," Elizabeth quipped as she followed Clare out the door.

With fumbling fingers that felt like lead weights, Elizabeth punched the numbers of her calling card into the phone on Burk's desk. She waited tensely for the phone in Trevor's office to ring while staring at the door, listening for Burk's footsteps outside. Burk always arrived promptly, and his note asked her to be here ten minutes from now.

"Hello," a brusque voice sounded impatiently through the receiver. Her call had obviously interrupted Trevor in the middle of something.

"Hello, Trevor . . . it's Elizabeth. Sorry to have caught you when you're busy." Twisting her fingers through the coiled cord of the phone, she waited for her fiancé to respond.

"Elizabeth?" his voice held a sharp edge of disbelief, mixed with irritation.

"Yes, Trevor. How are things there in New York?"

"Elizabeth, do you have any idea what time it is here?"

Of course she did. It was two hours later than here in Texas. "I'm sorry to be calling you at the office, Trevor, but I wanted to be sure to catch you. I know how much you hate being interrupted.''

''I see.''

She could sense his patience waning. ''How are—''

''It would be more convenient if you called back this evening. I'll have time to talk to you then.''

No! A wave of panic washed across her. This wasn't how she envisioned the call. Trevor should be talking to her when Burk walked in the door. That's how she wanted him to learn about her engagement to Trevor.

The thought of spending an uncomfortable day here with Burk was intolerable. Trying to avoid talking about what happened yesterday . . .

How would she manage to avoid his searching eyes? Or the furtive looks, like those she felt yesterday during the drive back from the ranch? It would be unendurable.

''I'm afraid I won't be able to call you later. Are you sure you don't have a moment to spare for me right now? It's very important to me, Trevor.''

''I suppose. But surely you realize now how much your little summer jaunt is inconveniencing both of us.''

Little summer jaunt? ''I'm sorry, Trevor. It's the only time I have, and I felt I needed to talk to you.''

''Yes.'' He paused long enough to sigh heavily. ''I'm sure you did. But next time I must insist you call at a more convenient hour, Elizabeth.''

''I will, I promise.''

''Now tell me what is so pressing that you had to bother me at the office.''

''Well, I just wanted to let you know my work here is

going very well. I'm getting along successfully with Dr. Sutherland, and he's told me I'm doing a commendable job.''

"And is this making you happy?"

Of course it made her happy! Elizabeth knotted her fingers tighter in the phone cord. This job turned out to be exactly what she needed. For the first time in her life she felt useful, necessary. Her love of archaeology, simply for the sake of learning, continued growing every day.

"I'm very happy," she insisted. "My work is so interesting, and Dr. Sutherland is a very intriguing man." Oh! She hadn't meant to say that!

"Is he?"

"I went on a trip to a canyon near here a couple of weeks ago. We had a great time."

"We? Was Dr. Sutherland with you?" Trevor's words were clipped and terse.

Just then the office door opened and Burk stepped in. Elizabeth felt her heart leap up into her throat and threaten to choke off her reply. "Yes," she finally managed. In a raw instant, she absorbed the sight of him, his lean frame in a chambray work shirt and faded jeans.

"And who else?"

Trevor kept speaking to her. By his tone, she knew he must be upset, but she couldn't think of the words she needed to calm his suspicions. Suspicions she could feel forming. "A friend."

Maybe it was only her guilty conscience. Maybe Trevor didn't suspect what she herself knew to be the truth. Something had indeed developed between her and Burk Sutherland.

"Elizabeth, I'm glad you called when you did."

She could hear a smile shading his tone now.

"I've been thinking that it might be a good idea to pay you a short visit, get a look at where you've been spending your time. I've missed you, you know."

She felt herself losing it again. Control of the conversation kept slipping away from her. She needed to let Burk know who she was talking to, then end this mess.

"I've missed you too, honey." She almost choked on the endearment. Never in their entire relationship had she ever called Trevor by anything other than his name. It felt so false to do so now. "But you'll see enough of me once we're married in December."

There! She did it. Elizabeth peered at Burk out of the corner of her eye. He stood by a filing cabinet, intently studying papers he had pulled from the drawers.

Darn. She couldn't tell if he'd been listening or not. There was no way she would be up to a repeat performance of those last two statements.

"But I'd feel better if I came out and paid you a short visit," Trevor continued.

Elizabeth's attention jolted from Burk's powerful form to Trevor's distant voice. "What? No—"

"Now, Elizabeth, I don't mind taking time out of my busy schedule to pay you a little visit, especially since I know how much it will mean to you."

"But, Trevor, I'm very busy right now. You shouldn't come all the way out here—"

"Your fiancé wants to come for a visit?" Burk's resonant tones startled her. He still stood at the filing cabinet, casually looking over his shoulder at her.

"Y—yes."

"Then by all means, Miss Way, invite him to come."

She stared at the smoky grayness of his eyes. They seemed to be hiding a fire within, and Elizabeth wondered what burned at the center of that fire. What possessed Burk to want her fiancé here, after the way he kissed her yesterday? Did this simply give her further proof of his regret over the kiss they shared?

All during the drive home she'd been painfully aware of his silence, of the tenseness that had flown up between them like a brick wall. At the time, she blamed it on her reaction to him. But he must be desperate, as desperate as she, to make sure that it never happened again.

The realization shook her to the bottom of her soul. Untangling her fingers from the phone cord, Elizabeth put her hand flat on Burk's desk to steady herself. She had to clear her head, to think calmly.

"I'll fly out this afternoon."

"What?" She tried to concentrate on Trevor's words. "This afternoon?"

Trevor didn't seem to notice her difficulty. He continued making his plans as if he were speaking to himself. Elizabeth tore her gaze from Burk's formidable features, painfully aware that his eyes were still locked on her. Distantly, she registered the fact that Trevor was ending the conversation, and she squeaked a frail good-bye before replacing the receiver.

Taking a cleansing breath, Elizabeth stood and marched over to her typing table, determined to appear calm while she felt Burk watching her.

"Would you like to take the day off to get ready for your fiancé's visit?"

"No," she answered calmly, fighting the urge to glare at him. "That won't be necessary, thank you." Elizabeth would show him she could be just as cold and indifferent about their kiss as he could.

"Would you like to get started on the next section of the book now? I have the notes typed up on the Archaic Period."

"Yes." His demeanor was purely business. "Let's get organized on the dart hunters."

For the next few hours they discussed the hunter-gatherer societies that lived around the Lubbock Lake Site during the six-thousand-year Archaic Period. Drought and increased heat changed the landscape of the region and the food sources available to the people.

Elizabeth tried to keep a clinical mind as she peered over Burk's shoulder while he explained his drawings of the desert plants that replaced the lush grass in the area. He showed her a drawing of the smaller buffalo that replaced the ancient, massive bison hunted by the people of the Paleo-Indian Period.

Listening to his passionate explanations of the changes the new climate caused, Elizabeth found herself lost in the color of his eyes, the movement of his lips. Several times during the day she used the excuse of needing a drink of water to get away from him for a few minutes, to bring her churning emotions under control.

By late evening, Elizabeth's nerves jangled raw. She felt in no mood to face Trevor when he phoned from the airport to tell her he would be arriving shortly to pick her up for dinner.

"Trevor will be here soon," she told Burk as she hung up the phone.

"Well, then you'd better hurry along and get ready." Burk shooed her to the door. "I'll see you tomorrow, and you needn't come in till noon, if you'd like," he generously offered.

Elizabeth forced a tremulous smile to her lips, and without a word slipped out the door, fuming all the way back to the small room she shared with Clare. She silently cursed her cowardice.

"This is where I spend most of my time," Elizabeth explained as she led Trevor into Burk's empty office the next morning. This early in the day she knew he would still be at the dig.

"Charming," Trevor commented dryly as he spared the cramped room a cursory glance.

Dispassionately she surveyed Trevor. His brown hair was trimmed to perfection, and combed neatly in place, flawlessly framing his ivy-league looks. Today he dressed the part of a casual tourist, in a turquoise, oxford shirt and chinos. The tasseled loafers wouldn't stand up to much of the trail dust though, Elizabeth silently observed.

"And what do you do in here?"

"Whatever Dr. Sutherland needs me to do," she answered distractedly, her eyes drifting over to the work piled up by her typewriter.

"I'd like to meet this Dr. Sutherland I've been hearing

so much about.'' Trevor stood by the door, his arms crossed over his chest.

''We'll probably run into him a little later—''

''I'd like to meet him now. You do know where he'd be, don't you?''

Closing here eyes, Elizabeth allowed herself to sigh, but it didn't help. Trevor could be a master at manipulating things to get what he wanted. Shortly after greeting Trevor last night, she'd gotten the impression that his main reason for coming to Texas was to see Burk Sutherland.

''Sure.'' She tried to sound cheerful about his request. After all, she had nothing to hide, right? Turning to the door, she said, ''He'll be at the dig, and I'd planned to show you that next, so why don't we get to it?''

''Let's do that,'' Trevor said as he followed her out the door. ''Dr. Sutherland may be a busy man, but I doubt he'll mind taking time from his work to visit with me. A professional man usually likes explaining his work to another man who's capable of understanding him.''

Capable of understanding! If that was his subtle way of putting her in her place, Elizabeth decided it was none too subtle. She fumed as she led Trevor down the trail to the site where she saw Burk hard at work, brushing sediment away from his latest finds. Pausing nearby, she suddenly felt a strong sense of dread, and knew she was about to make a terrible mistake, but the decision about introducing Trevor to Burk got taken out of her hands.

''Dr. Sutherland? Trevor brushed past her, offering his hand to the man kneeling on the ground. ''Trevor Davis, Elizabeth's fiancé.''

She hung back, not wanting to be any part of the conversation between the two men. Why had her phone call ended up producing results like this? Trevor didn't belong here. He wasn't a part of her life here in Texas. He belonged back in New York with her parents, with what she had come to think of as her old life, a life she felt so far removed from now.

Chapter Seven

" "I'll be spending another night here, then it's back to New York for me, I'm afraid. Elizabeth will have to get along without me."

Trevor's voice grated across her ear as he spoke with Burk. She wanted to run and run, but she had no place to go. So, she stood a few feet away from the two men, and waited for Trevor to run out of steam. Funny, she never thought of him that way before, as a big bag of hot air.

But, maybe her thoughts about Trevor were too harsh. The problem could be that Burk was so close, that she couldn't help comparing the two men. She seemed to be rapidly finding out that there could be no man who would stand up in comparison with Burk Sutherland.

"I'm planning to take your little assistant out to a decent restaurant for lunch, before I allow her to get back to digging in the dirt today, old man. Hope you don't mind."

And what if he does mind, she wanted to shout. What then, Trevor?

"Of course not," Burk beamed at Trevor. "Take all the time you need."

Unable to bear another minute of Trevor's cavalier treatment, Elizabeth spun on her heel and marched back to Burk's office. Seating herself in front of the typewriter, she worked feverishly, trying to finish as many pages as possible before Trevor found her again. She knew she would go to lunch with him, without objection. She always did what Trevor wanted.

Well, almost always, she reminded herself with a secret smile. She had come here over his objections. But his disapproval hadn't been as strong as her parents'; in fact, Trevor never expressed very strong feelings about anything connected with her. She tried to clear her mind of thoughts of her fiancé, and concentrate on the work in front of her. At least she could be of some help to Burk today, even if he hadn't seemed particularly concerned about how she spent her time.

Two hours passed before Trevor swept into the office and, without a word, ushered her into the Mercedes-Benz he'd rented for his short stay here.

Numbly, Elizabeth sat across from Trevor in the posh, downtown restaurant, half-heartedly listening to him dissect her job.

"He seems like a competent man, and I'm sure you enjoy your work, otherwise you wouldn't stay. Am I right, Elizabeth?" Trevor tapped his fork lightly against a tall wine glass, sharply drawing her attention.

"Yes, Trevor, he's very nice." She took a small sip of her white wine, and found it bitter.

"I see. Elizabeth," he pursed his lips as he paused. "How well has Dr. Sutherland been treating you?"

"Very well," she answered, her graceful eyebrows arched at his curious question. "Why do you ask?"

"I've been a bit concerned." He rocked back in his chair, gazing steadily at her.

She'd been right! It wasn't just her guilty conscience telling her Trevor suspected that something happened between her and Burk. "Well you needn't be," she lied. "He treats me like a professional." At least that was the truth.

"A professional what?"

"Trevor!" distress elevated Elizabeth's voice, as her hands flew up to cover her flaming cheeks.

"He's a learned man, Elizabeth, quite accomplished. What can he possibly see in you?" he continued, completely unconcerned about her distress.

"Dr. Sutherland is a dedicated scholar. He's devoted to archaeology. In me, he sees an educated professional, who's willing to put in the long hours the job demands, just as he is!" She felt light-headed and paused to draw a deep breath.

"But it's just a hobby with you. I'm sorry to be the one to tell you this, but I don't think Dr. Sutherland's interest in you is all that professional." Trevor turned his back on her and signaled to the white-jacketed waiter. Handing the young man a credit card, he snapped, "Make it quick, we're ready to leave."

Elizabeth stared down at her almost-untouched food. The braised lamb and endives lay in the congealed Mornay sauce. As usual, Trevor had ordered for her without consulting her, forgetting that she detested lamb.

"I spent a very informative morning with the man," Trevor continued as they stepped out of the restaurant. "I have to say, my intuition was right on the money about him."

Always the gentleman, Trevor held the car door open for her, but Elizabeth managed to slide in without touching his outstretched hand. Joining her inside, he continued, "He's only interested in one thing from you, Elizabeth."

"Trevor, I think you're wrong."

"I'm not wrong about that man's motives. There's only one reason you still have that job." He smirked derisively at her as he started the car and left the restaurant.

"Burk treats me like an educated professional," she repeated desperately. "He's interested in my abilities as an assistant, nothing more."

Did she hear an echo of regret in her last two words? She felt the tingling warmth Burk's lips had left on hers when he kissed her. Her words might have been a lie. . . . But no, she remembered all too clearly the regret that shone in his eyes after that kiss. Burk completely withdrew during the drive back from Jess's ranch to the Lubbock Lake Site. Then, during her phone call, he so eagerly assured her that her fiancé should come visit. That memory still felt like a raw wound in her mind.

"I am an educated professional, Trevor. And that's all Burk sees in me. That's what he appreciates about me. I'm qualified for the job, and that's why I still have it." Only when she stopped did she realize she had been shouting. The confining space of the car's interior left her ears ringing.

"You're the one who's wrong, Elizabeth. He couldn't possibly see those qualities in you. He has no idea you're the least bit qualified for the job you're doing."

Trevor stopped the car and Elizabeth realized that he had driven her to his hotel. He stepped out, and she clambered out also, without waiting for him to open her door. Her haste made her awkward. "What do you mean?" she demanded. "Of course he does." She dogged his steps all the way to his suite. "Burk received a copy of my application from Wally. It listed all of my education and my experience at the American Museum of Natural History. In case you're not aware of what I did there, Trevor, it's a lot like what I do for Burk."

Trevor spared her a pitying glance as he unlocked the door and sauntered in. "Yes, I'm well aware of the qualifications listed on your application. If you'll remember, I came by your parent's penthouse the day you finished typing it up for Wally," he said as he calmly crossed the spacious room and poured himself a drink at the fully stocked bar.

"Yes," she replied wrinkling her forehead in concentration, "you were. Why are you telling me all this? Why are you trying to insinuate Burk shouldn't think I'm qualified for the job?"

"Elizabeth, come sit here with me," he indicated the cream and gold sofa by the bar. When she joined him he stared levelly into her eyes. "I knew this job was all wrong for my future wife, and so did your parents, if you'll remember."

"I know you have objections, but this is something I really want to do," she stressed.

"Yes, but that doesn't necessarily make it right. Does it, Elizabeth?"

"Trevor—"

"Sometimes I know what's better for you than you do. Can't you admit that?"

"I think—"

"It really doesn't matter what you think, Elizabeth." He was losing his patience with her. "This whole thing is a bad idea, and Wally was a fool to even consider allowing you to take a job. I hope your parents realize he's no true friend of theirs."

"How can you possibly say that about Wally?"

"Never mind about Wally! His role in this fiasco is insignificant now. All you need to be concerned with is Dr. Sutherland's motives in keeping you in a position he knows you are unqualified for."

"But I'm not," she protested. "Why do you keep saying that?" Tears threatened to form in the corners of her eyes, but Elizabeth willed them away.

"As far as your Dr. Sutherland knows, you aren't qualified." He returned to the bar and poured himself another drink. "Do you remember my offering to mail your application for you? I was leaving when you finished it, and said I'd drop it off in the lobby of your apartment building."

"Yes, of course I remember that, Trevor." At the time she had been thrilled by the offer. It seemed like a stamp of approval from him on a subject that hadn't been pleasant for him.

"I didn't mail it right away, Elizabeth. I took it back to my office and made a few changes first."

"Changes?"

Trevor held a hand up to forestall her questions. "Changes that were for your own good, I assure you. This is a silly notion, and it has been from the very beginning. I saw an easy way to convince you that I was right. I knew that if Dr. Sutherland received an assistant he knew to be unqualified, he'd send them back. Or at the very least, not be very welcoming to them."

That's what Burk had done that first day, she realized. He tried his hardest to make her feel unwelcome. He tried to overwhelm her with the amount of work he would expect of her. He even suggested she leave.

"But, he didn't do that. Did he?" Trevor loomed over her, trying to draw an answer out of her. "He got one look at you and decided he could make use of you in another way."

"What? No! Trevor—"

"He saw a young, rich girl, with a pretty face, and decided she might be good for a 'roll in the hay', as they say around here."

"No, Trevor, you're wrong." She felt the return of the tears that threatened to fall earlier. It wasn't true, she knew. Yet, she couldn't deny the passion she'd felt in the sole kiss they shared. And she felt guilt.

"I'm right, Elizabeth. There's no way he could have kept you for any other reason. To him, you're nothing more than a dabbling amateur history buff, a play-toy for his amusement."

Pressing the heels of her hands against her stinging eyes, Elizabeth fought for a calmer tone of voice. "What did you do, Trevor?" she asked flatly. "What did you do to my application?"

"Not much, really. I just used a bit of correction fluid, till I had a blank form. Then I copied it on my machine, and started over."

"Started over?" Repeating his words seemed to be a habit she was forming. They were so incredible, she couldn't believe what she heard.

"I filled out most of the personal data just as you had. But I left out your college degree, and your experience at the museum. The changes were for your own good," he repeated.

"I expected you to come rushing back to New York, where you belong. But after a few weeks, I decided you might be all right here. Then I received that disturbing phone call from you, and realized something must be wrong."

He erased her qualifications? This time she managed to keep from repeating his words out loud. Elizabeth sank back against the cushions of the couch, needing their support.

"I am correct, aren't I, Elizabeth? Something is wrong here."

Yes. Something is terribly wrong. "You expected Burk to reject me as his assistant. You expected me to come running back to you."

"That's what I expected to happen. Then I heard a peculiar note in your voice when you talked about Dr. Sutherland. I knew something must be up." He sat back down beside her with a full drink.

"I see," she said slowly. It became impossible to think. What could she say to the man who just revealed how he betrayed her, how he sabotaged the one thing she wanted in the world? "You didn't want me to succeed here. You wanted me to see what a bad choice I made when I decided to go against your wishes."

"And you did make a bad choice. I hope you see that now." He patted her knee.

"I see that I've made many bad choices, Trevor."

"But allowing yourself to become an object of Dr. Sutherland's sexual interest has to have been the worst choice you've ever made, isn't it, Elizabeth?" he asked ruthlessly. Trevor wasn't used to her responding to his influence this way. He didn't like it.

Yesterday had been a mistake, she knew. Things had changed between them as a result of that kiss. Burk saw her differently now. Did he see her as some young amateur, following him around like a love-sick puppy? And it was true. He had treated her differently when he thought she was younger, much younger than him.

"Trevor, did you change my age too?" she surprised herself with how calm she managed to sound.

"What does it matter?" he asked, irritation coloring his words. The glass in his hand was empty again.

"Did you?" she persisted.

"Yes, I did. But that doesn't matter now, I tell you. What matters is what we choose to do about Dr. Sutherland's unprofessional conduct."

"To what?" she pressed him for an answer. "What did you change my age to?"

"Nineteen." Glowering at his glass, Trevor rose and re-filled it.

"Nineteen!" And she practically yelled at Burk for treating her as if she were so much younger than he. Now she

knew why he seemed so shocked when she informed him
of her right age. She could clearly recall the comical expression on his face. Somewhere halfway between befud-
dled and stunned. But she made him believe it. Despite
what he read on her application, he took her word for it
when she confronted him with her true age.

Elizabeth smiled at the memory of his expression.

''Do you think this is funny?'' Trevor's face flushed with
a frown. ''I'll have you know we should add cradle-robbing
to the list of Dr. Sutherland's transgressions. Why, I've half
a mind to call up the money people who back his research
and have the man stripped of his funding. I'm not without
influence in certain circles, you know.''

''What? Take away his funding?'' She sprang to her feet.

''Absolutely.'' Trevor leaned on the glass counter of the
bar. ''It's the least that lecher deserves for making a play
for my fiancée.''

''No, Trevor!'' Panic tightened her throat.

''Yes, I think I'll take care of Dr. Sutherland the first
thing in the morning.''

''No.'' She had to think fast. ''No, Trevor, you've got
it all wrong. Dr. Sutherland isn't the one.'' That stopped
him, she saw, with satisfaction. ''You were right about one
thing. I have fallen in love with another man.''

Turning her back on Trevor, Elizabeth paced across the
room to the window. ''But it isn't Burk. The man I love is
a rancher. He lives near here.'' Glancing at Trevor, she
could tell that he was stunned, too stunned to recognize the
web of lies she kept spinning. ''His name is Jess. He and
I have been seeing each other almost every day. In fact, I

spent the evening at his place, the day before I phoned you.''

Confidence filtered into Elizabeth as she approached Trevor again. He gaped silently at her, then took a long swallow from his glass.

''I phoned you to break off our engagement, because Jess has asked me to marry him.'' Elizabeth was amazed. She'd put together an outlandish string of lies, and it looked as if Trevor was buying every one of them.

''I'm going to live on the ranch with him, and raise horses. It's not a very big place, a two-bedroom house and a couple of barns. But we don't need much. You see, we're in love.''

Trevor grew white around his eyes. The pallor stood out in a terrible contrast to the cherry red of his nose and cheeks. It actually looked to her as if he were swaying a little. She took a step back, hoping the shock and all the liquor would do the job she wanted to do; to knock him down. If so, she didn't want to be in the position of breaking his fall. And it looked like it would be quite a fall for Trevor Davis.

For probably the first time in his sanctimonious life, a woman was jilting him. And jilting him hard. Well, he deserved what he got, she mused. How she wanted to scream, to spit in his face. But she couldn't, not without jeopardizing Burk's career. So Elizabeth kept the truth of her feelings for Burk locked safely inside.

''But . . . what about us? What about my father's business?''

Finally Trevor let the truth of the matter out in the open!

He was upset about the loss to his business that the ending of their engagement would mean.

"I don't know, Trevor. I can't be troubled with thinking about business at a time like this, my thoughts are full of Jess. We're a match made in heaven."

The irony struck her at once. These were almost the exact words she'd heard from her mother, just before leaving New York, back when she thought Trevor really loved her.

Now Elizabeth knew what troubled her so much about her impending marriage. It had no love in it.

"I'll forgive you, Elizabeth. We'll forget this summer ever happened." Trevor seemed to be sobering up, and realizing he was losing something he counted on to ease his taking control of the company when his father retired.

"Oh, that's wonderful of you, Trevor. But it's too late."

"Too late? Of course it isn't too late," he blustered.

"Yes, I'm afraid it is. You see, we've set a date, we've told his family," she shrugged casually, "his friends."

Choking out incoherent gasps, Trevor stumbled around behind the bar, searching for another bottle. After refilling his glass he set the bottle back on the shelf. Then, changing his mind, he retrieved the bottle and carried it to the sofa.

"We'll be married next month on a Sunday." Elizabeth couldn't help herself, she was starting to have fun now. "The flowers and my dress have been ordered. Everything will be so perfect. But it's time for me to get back, Trevor. I have so much to do."

Still reeling from the news, Trevor mumbled something about giving her a ride back to the archaeological dig. Elizabeth graciously declined, suggesting that he should stay and rest, she could catch a cab. While he was in a fog, she slipped his keys off the table by the door and dropped them in her purse. After saying a quick good-bye, Elizabeth left Trevor's car keys with the clerk at the front desk and had him call a cab for her.

All the way back to the dig, she congratulated herself on doing such a masterful job of handling Trevor. But when the elm trees that circled the lake site came into view, Elizabeth's spirits began to sink. Now she had to face the tough decision of what to do next. Somehow there had to be a way out of the mess she was in with Burk.

"Trevor's leaving this morning," she told Burk as they walked from the compound to the dig.

"Of course, you'll want some time off to see him to the airport." His tone was terse.

"No. We said our good-byes after lunch yesterday."

Burk pounded down the trail, his hands clenching and unclenching. "But if you'd like some time off—"

"No." She tried not to sound as tense as Burk sounded, but it seemed almost impossible. Somehow, today, Elizabeth intended to get a look at what Trevor had done to her application. He'd erased her education and work experience, even changed her age.

It all seemed so impossible, she had to see it for herself. She had to hold it in her hand, not to make herself believe he could do it, but to put an end to her relationship with Trevor in her mind. She had no doubt they were through. But somehow, it seemed all too unreal. How could he have thought he could manipulate her like that and get away with it? Shaking her head, she resolved to put Trevor out of her thoughts. Right now, she should be concentrating on Dr. Sutherland, and her job.

"Do you have many notes for me to type on the Archaic Period?"

"What? Yes," he answered distractedly, his eyes taking a moment to focus on her. "Yes, we'll get started on them after lunch."

"If you don't have to be at the dig this morning, you could get your notes ready now, couldn't you? I mean, I could do the work at the dig by myself."

It was the first time she suggested he let her do the excavating alone. Part of his grant requirements was that he spend a certain amount of time at the task of excavating the area around Lubbock Lake, she knew. But he had spent more than enough time there, she believed. He also wanted to be finished with a certain area, before his time here ended. The excavating should be something she could handle alone now, just as Jean-Paul had.

"No." He quickly rebuffed her offer.

"I can do the job, Burk," she assured him.

Would this be a good time to tell him what had been done to her application? No, she decided. She didn't want Burk to know what Trevor had done to her. The thought of him seeing how gullible she'd been, what a fool she'd been, left her cold. And if he knew what Trevor had done, he would also realize she'd broken off her engagement.

The one thing she regretted about her confrontation with Trevor was that her ring was still in New York. A melodramatic scene popped into her mind of herself throwing the ring at Trevor's feet.

The wedding preparations should be canceled as soon as possible, she realized. During her lunch break, some calls would have to be made to New York. The housekeeper could send Trevor's ring to his home immediately. Hopefully, it would be waiting for him when he arrived back there. It wasn't as melodramatic as throwing the ring at his feet, but it would do. She grinned at the satisfying picture that made.

Glancing at the man beside her, Elizabeth realized he'd been studying her intently. The silly grin instantly grew stiff on her face and melted off as Burk's heated gaze intensified. They both stopped on the trail, watching each other expectantly. She could see his chest heaving in and out with each deep breath. His lips parted slightly, just enough to allow a glimmer of his even, white teeth to show.

Nervously, she ran a tongue across her dry lips, and found them tingling with anticipation. The memory of that one, too-brief kiss they shared on horseback came rushing into her mind. Gradually the realization dawned on her that Burk was staring at her mouth, watching the nervous flick of her tongue across her red lips.

Something had to break the tension she felt building between them. She cleared her throat, and felt it tighten. Moving back from him seemed like a good idea. Maybe then her mind could start functioning again. Blindly, she stepped back, and felt her foot slide out from under her as it landed on a rock.

Like a panther, Burk leaped forward and caught her before she struck the ground. His arms felt as unyielding as steel cables as he supported her weight effortlessly. Elizabeth gazed up into his mysterious, smoky eyes, and felt an overpowering urge to sink into their depth. Her hands clung to his broad shoulders, her fingers twining into the rough fabric of his pale blue shirt. The enticingly masculine scent of him threatened to overpower her senses as she froze in his solid embrace.

With a touch as light as a feather, Elizabeth sensed Burk trail his fingers down her arm, then press his hand into the small of her back. The trembling in her ribs spread up to her lips. What could he be thinking? Did he want to kiss her?

Voices drifted down the trail, followed by the sound of footsteps. She struggled to right herself before whoever she heard approaching came into view. Burk realized what Elizabeth was doing, and loosened his hold on her, allowing her to gain her balance. Then he stepped back a respectable distance from her just as two college students, volunteers here for the summer, rounded a bend in the trail.

''Hello, Dr. Sutherland, Miss Way,'' one of them called a greeting.

Elizabeth managed a smile in return, while Burk gave them a curt nod.

Falling into step behind the students, she listened for Burk's footsteps. Without a word, he followed close behind, close enough to make her heart race with his nearness.

The sun shone high overhead as Elizabeth knelt beside the unit Burk excavated. Drops of perspiration formed on her forehead. Burk labored like a man driven to finish a task, or die trying. This couldn't go on much longer, she swore silently as she shifted her notes restlessly in her hands. The tension that grew between them would have to be stopped, or they would both go insane!

''Elizabeth!'' a woman's voice jarred her from her trance-like state.

Looking around, she saw Clare hurrying toward her.

"Your fiancé is here looking for you," her roommate announced as she halted to peer over Elizabeth's shoulder. "He's back at the compound."

"Trevor's here?" Oh no! A sense of apprehension washed over her. "What does he want? Did he say?"

"Probably to kiss you good-bye, silly."

No. He couldn't want that. Not after the way they parted. This could be real trouble. Or, maybe he had just come for the ring. She hadn't taken the time to tell him she'd left it in New York. Hopefully that was all he wanted.

"Well? Don't you want to go see him?" Clare asked.

Elizabeth stared mutely up at her friend, then, with dread, turned to Burk. He stared at her, his mouth stretched in a tight line. She needed to ask him if she could leave for a few minutes, but her mouth had suddenly gone too dry to form any sounds.

"Go ahead," Burk said. "I can finish up here without you."

Burk's words fell on her ears like shards of broken glass.

Chapter Eight

Scrambling to her feet, Elizabeth tried not to hurry as she struck out down the trail. She tried swallowing to clear her throat of the lump that began to form there, but didn't succeed before reaching the compound. Trevor stood on the edge of the clearing, leaning against a tall elm tree.

"What is it?" she demanded, marching briskly up to him. "I thought we'd said all we needed to say yesterday at your hotel."

"Hello," he said, almost jauntily, as he tried one of his winning smiles on her. "Just wanted a quick word. I promise not to take up too much of your time."

She had seen women melt when given one of those smiles from Trevor, but today, it made her blood run cold. "Well?" Balling her fists, she planted them on her hips.

"Actually," he began quietly, as his eyes drifted down to the ground where he traced circles in the dust with the toe of his shoe. "I've come to apologize."

"Why?" Wariness caused her to take a step back. She shouldn't trust anything he might say. He would have some ulterior motive; Trevor always did.

"I was terribly wrong. I should never have changed your application. I realize that now, that I was wrong about you and Dr. Sutherland."

But he hadn't been wrong. Something had happened between her and Burk. At least, for her it had. And she still felt it, whatever it was. Burk obviously regretted the kiss they shared. His silence made that evident to her. Elizabeth stared at Trevor, keeping her thoughts locked inside.

"Yesterday, it seemed to me that he had some kind of a hang-up on you. I don't exactly know what gave me that idea, it was just a suspicion I had. That, coupled with the feeling that you were interested in him . . . '' He took a deep breath. "Now I know I was wrong, but I also know that doesn't change anything between us." Trevor shuffled his feet and nervously shifted his gaze back and forth between the ground and Elizabeth.

"No, it doesn't, Trevor. We're through, and it doesn't really matter who came between us. That isn't what ended our relationship."

"Right," he agreed.

"Right?" she asked, her eyes widening with skepticism. For the first time, Trevor agreed with her opinion, even though it differed from his own.

"This Jess guy; he could never have come between us if we were really meant to be together. Something just went wrong somewhere, Elizabeth. Somewhere along the line, we lost touch, we lost our mutual goal of a future together."

"Yes." Probably the second she first caught sight of Burk Sutherland, she berated herself. But Trevor's words rang true. They did want a future together at one time, she believed. What she could clearly see now was that they never really understood what each other expected out of that future. Trevor never truly knew what she wanted to do with her life, and she had to accept that now.

She felt guilty for allowing him to have control of her direction, to plan her future, to determine her goals. Elizabeth shivered involuntarily. From now on, she would be the master of her destiny.

"Anyway," he stood straighter and finally looked her in the eye, "I wanted to see if it would be possible for us to end our engagement, but not our friendship. I trust we can stay friends. I mean, if we happen to bump into each other at the theater, or at a party?" he finished on a hopeful note.

That would be virtually impossible if she were really staying in Texas to marry Jess, she mused. What could Trevor be thinking about? What was he really after?

"Our families could even do a business deal together someday. Don't you think that might be possible?"

So much raw hope echoed in his voice that Elizabeth almost laughed in his face. Almost. But her mother had ingrained better manners in her than that. "I suppose so, Trevor. It's possible our families will still have a cooperative business relationship. That is, if we manage to end our engagement amicably."

"Y—yes," he stammered eagerly. "I think that's best, I really do." He reached for her hand and she let him pat it reassuringly.

"But there are two things I want, Trevor." Elizabeth pulled her hand from his as an idea formed in her mind.

"Yes, Elizabeth, anything. Just tell me what they are."

"First, I want no mention of your changing my application, not ever again," she told him sternly. "Never."

"Not even to Dr. Sutherland?" he asked. "You don't want me to straighten out the mess I've put you in with him?"

"Absolutely not." That was the last thing she wanted. What would Burk think of her if he found out what Trevor had done to her? She never wanted him to know that she had been so easily manipulated by this man. More important, she didn't want him to know of her broken engagement. She needed a buffer between them, and an engagement, even a false one, would work perfectly.

Despite all his faults, Trevor did help her understand one thing more clearly. Burk did think of her as nothing more than an uneducated, inexperienced amateur. He kissed her. He kissed her, when he really had no feelings for her. Otherwise, why would he have shunned her since then? That was the most damning evidence yet.

"I'll take care of my slight problem with Dr. Sutherland. And the second thing I want from you, Trevor; don't mention Jess or my involvement with him to my parents, or anyone else. I think it's best if we just say we've decided we're not right for each other. That's somewhat close to the truth. Don't you think so?"

"Yes, absolutely," he agreed. "And I can tell your father that we still think our families would benefit from a mutually cooperative business relationship, can't I?"

"Mutually cooperative sounds good to me, Trevor. But

wait until I talk to Daddy first.'' Perhaps if her father felt he hadn't lost any business opportunities over his daughter's rash actions he would be more likely to accept her decision without an argument.

''Oh, Elizabeth,'' Trevor gushed as he pulled her into an embrace. ''You're such a wonderful girl.'' He squeezed her tight, then planted an enthusiastic kiss on her lips.

Elizabeth jerked her head back in surprise, but his firm embrace held her immobile against his chest. When his grip finally relaxed, she stepped back in amazement, her hand flying to her lips.

''Things will work out fine between us, you'll see. And I wish you all the happiness in the world with Jess.'' He had allowed her to slide out of his embrace, but caught the hand that wasn't pressed to her mouth. ''I'll call you in a few days to check on the cancellation of the wedding plans.''

''Sure, that'll be fine, Trevor. Just remember your promise to me. Not a word about—''

''Not a word. I promise. And if there's ever anything you need—''

''I'll call,'' she said, knowing that she never would.

''Well, I'd better go, I don't want to miss my flight.''

''Good-bye, Trevor.''

''Good-bye, Elizabeth,'' he said as he finally released her hand. ''And good luck.''

As he walked away, Elizabeth searched inside herself for any signs of regret over the end of their relationship. Smiling with a new sense of resolve, she realized that she had none.

*　　*　　*

A satisfied smile graced Elizabeth's lips, Burk saw. He stood there, on the edge of the compound, under the shade of one of the towering elm trees, the same spot he'd stood in for the last three minutes. Elizabeth and her fiancé were deep in an intense discussion when Burk first arrived. At this distance it was impossible for him to tell what they were talking about.

Then, he kissed her. Trevor swept her supple form into his embrace, and kissed her. Burk squeezed his eyes shut, remembering the feel of Elizabeth's lips molded to his own. He longed to take her in his arms again, to taste the soft sweetness of her. The desire became a dull ache deep in his soul.

As Trevor walked out of sight, Burk shifted his raw stare back to Elizabeth. She turned around. Their eyes locked, as if welded together. There was nothing he could do, his body refused to obey his command to leave. He drank in the sight of her elated face; her lips, parted and flushed from Trevor's enthusiastic kiss, her hazel eyes, sparkling with some inner secret. She looked satisfied.

Could he ever make her feel that way? Could he ever sweep her into his embrace and kiss her until she looked just as contented? He ached with a longing to try. But he didn't have the right to.

Elizabeth held his gaze for a moment, then resolutely turned away. A trace of stiffness showed in her walk as she paced to the low office building nearby. When she was inside, out of his sight, Burk felt his muscles come to life again. He shook his head in bewilderment, then followed her, determined to get to work and keep his desires under tight control from now until she left Texas. The closer he got to his office door, the more impossible that task seemed.

The rhythmic tickings of Elizabeth's fingers on the type-writer keys filled the small office. Burk worked at his draft-ing table, seemingly oblivious to her presence, just as he had for the last five days since Trevor's visit. Despite the outward appearance of calm, she felt an uneasiness every time they worked closely.

"Do you want to get some dinner with me before we tackle these first pages on the Archaic Period?" Burk asked.

The rhythm faltered as her fingers fumbled over the keys. Elizabeth looked up in surprise. Five days with barely a word from him, and now he invites her to dinner?

"Sure," she agreed, doing her best to appear unruffled. "I'm getting hungry." With a little bit of determination it shouldn't be too hard for them to have a simple meal to-gether. Those silly feelings she had for Burk were firmly under control now. Dinner shouldn't be a problem at all.

"How about burgers? There's this little place I know of by the university. It used to be a florist's greenhouse."

"Sounds interesting," she agreed with a curious lift of her eyebrow. That was one place she hadn't heard about from Clare. It seemed that her roommate must be the most informed person about unusual or offbeat places of enter-tainment or eating within at least a fifty-mile radius of the dig. Now Elizabeth would have a place to report to Clare about. Although, leaving out the detail of who she went with might be a good idea.

Half an hour later they were seated across from one another at a small table. Quietly chatting diners crowded the rustic, stucco and exposed timber room. The ceiling high overhead was all skylights and rough beams, and Elizabeth became aware of the fading sunlight as they waited for their meal to arrive.

"I hope you're enjoying the work here this summer." Burk leaned across the table so his low voice would carry over the Huey Louis song drifting from the speakers in the corners of the room.

"Absolutely." Elizabeth tried not to babble. "I've gotten a lot out of my time here so far, and I can't wait to see your book in print."

"You're not the only one." Burk chuckled.

It felt so natural for Elizabeth to smile at him. All the tension that built between her shoulders from the long hours of typing today seeped away. "I see it's still quite important to you, even after all the articles you've published before."

"That's the truth! I always feel good about seeing my work in print. But this one means more to me than any thing I've ever written before."

"Because it will get you that job in Peru?"

"Yes. It's what I want more than anything. A position like that is what I've worked so hard for the last few years. I won't let anything stand in my way."

Not even an unqualified assistant, she reflected. But, he had let her stay, despite her seeming lack of qualifications. What was his motive behind that decision?

Could it be his interest in her personally, just as Trevor thought? Maybe at first. Yes, that must have been the reason. That would mean he wanted to kiss her as much as she wanted to kiss him that day at Jess's ranch. But after that disastrous kiss, why would he keep her here? Could he still be drawn to her, as she was to him?

If that were true, she wouldn't know whether to be angry or happy about it. It would mean he was attracted to her, but did he respect her? Oh, it all confused her so much.

"And what do you want to do with your future, Elizabeth? Do you want to continue working in some field of archaeology?"

"Yes, absolutely." And just like Burk had said a moment earlier, nothing would stand in her way. She would get another job when this one was over. No more living at home with her parents. No more languishing about, doing a little volunteer work, and living for parties, or charity functions like her mother and so many of her friends.

"Will you continue working after your marriage to Trevor?"

The question startled her. She'd been on the verge of letting her secret slip out. "I'm not going to quit working," she answered vaguely. "It'll probably be somewhere back east."

"Have you thought about getting formal training? Maybe going to college? With your experience this summer, and with your abilities, you'd make an excellent archaeologist. I mean it," he insisted when she blushed.

"I will admit that I've thought about what it would be like, trying to run an archaeological site. Honestly, I don't think it's for me."

He smiled with her. "But you do enjoy field work, don't you?"

"Yes, definitely. To tell you the truth," she hesitated,

smiling timidly, "I've actually thought about the position of administrative assistant to a director."

"Really?" Burk leaned back, his mouth open in surprise.

"I like the idea of being the person responsible for all the little mundane tasks that really keep a dig going. Things like getting equipment and supplies, arranging transportation and schedules. I'd even like to be in charge of the hiring and payroll."

"You would?"

"Yes. Why are you so surprised?"

Their waiter arrived with large platters of food. Delicious smells wafted to Elizabeth's nose, and she had to wait for Burk's answer, until they'd both taken a bite of their hamburgers. The food had been cooked over a fire of mesquite wood, which gave it a tantalizingly tangy flavor.

"I'm surprised because I never thought of you as the ambitious type," Burk mumbled between bites of food. "It simply never occurred to me. . . . "

"That I might like the responsibility?"

He didn't answer for some time. He studied her, watching the light dance off her hair. "I suppose there's a lot about you that I don't know, Elizabeth Way, but I intend to learn."

She smiled at his oddly worded phrase. Did he mean it as a warning, or a promise? "What about you, Burk? It's obvious to me that you like your work. But how did you get into it?"

"My father." He smiled at a memory. "He's a surgeon, just as his father was before him."

"I don't understand."

"He wanted to be a lawyer," Burk explained. "My dad

loved the idea of trying a case, of arguing his viewpoint, and winning. So, he made sure I pursued anything I even remotely became interested in when I was a child. It made life a bit chaotic at times, and my mother tried to put a stop to it more than once. Especially after some of my near-disasters. One time I decided I should be a chemist. I singed most of my hair off and almost burned down the garage.''

Elizabeth laughed at the image of Burk as a mischievous boy. He seemed to be enjoying the memories so much, she felt drawn into his joy. ''I can see you have a devilish side.''

''It wasn't all so disastrous. I did decide on a career that suits me perfectly. My dad knew what he was doing.'' Burk nodded his head for emphasis, then took a long drink of his iced tea. ''He made my childhood adventurous.''

''Oh, that sounds wonderful,'' she said softly. ''I wish mine had been more like yours.''

''Tell me about your childhood, Elizabeth,'' Burk said, reaching across the small table and lightly stroking her fingers. His gaze became intent, his smoky gray eyes locked on to her, searching her face earnestly.

''I grew up in Manhattan. There isn't much else to tell,'' she answered vaguely.

''What did you like to do when you were a child?''

Burk gently encouraged her to open up to him, and she saw what he was doing. For him, she would try. ''I liked going to all the museums,'' she answered almost hopefully. ''Do you think that's a strange thing for a young girl to want to do?''

''Not at all. Especially since the young girl we're talking

about is you. What did you dream of becoming when you grew up?''

''A pilot. Or a famous explorer.''

Burk laughed softly, his gentle stroking of her hand changing into a possessive hold. ''Quite the tomboy, I imagine.''

''Not at all,'' she denied. ''My mother would never have permitted the least unladylike activity from her daughter. I learned early to keep my true feelings to myself.''

''Is that what you're doing now? Keeping your true feelings secret?''

That was entirely too close for comfort, she realized. Cautiously, she pulled her hand from his, and took a drink of tea. The glass had sat untouched for so long, that the tea tasted weak from the melted ice. Grimacing from the taste, she quickly took a bite of her burger, filling her mouth with the wonderful mesquite flavoring, and making it impossible for her to answer Burk's probing question.

Burk followed her lead and attacked his meal with renewed vigor. For such a big man, it seemed to Elizabeth as if he ate very little. Yet there was no end to his energy; she could personally attest to that. He was such an intense man, and that feeling of intensity spread to her every time they were together.

''How about something for dessert?'' he asked, after swallowing the last bit of food on his plate.

''Oh, no,'' Elizabeth almost groaned. ''I couldn't eat another bite.''

Burk signaled their waiter for the check, and soon they were outside.

''I can't believe how much I ate,'' Elizabeth said as she

glanced back over her shoulder at the ivy-covered doorway they'd just walked through. "The food was incredible, Burk." She gazed up into his eyes as he linked his arm through hers. "I've had a marvelous time this evening."

"Then let's not let it end yet," he implored her. "How about a walk? You don't feel like dessert now, but after a walk you might. And I know of a great ice cream shop over on the campus." He pointed, indicating the tree-lined expanse across the street. Brick buildings, with Spanish-style red tile roofs, were interspersed graciously among the trees. "How about it, Elizabeth?"

It tempted her, the thought of strolling under the towering elms. The breeze felt wonderful on her skin. It would be a shame not to enjoy the cool evening air, she mused. And to do it in the company of this man. . . .

"All right," she agreed, realizing that it wasn't the most gracious of acceptances. To make up for her nervous lack of manners, Elizabeth smiled broadly at him.

She felt Burk's arm slip from hers, then circle around her back to nestle her closer. He kept her there as they crossed the wide street to the campus, then slid his hand away and down her arm to loosely clasp her hand.

They wandered along in easy silence to the large fountain near the main campus entrance, and stopped to study the marble carving of the university seal. It stood several feet taller than Burk, and Elizabeth was again reminded of his indomitable size.

Imposing would be a good word to describe Burk. Somber at times, she reflected, but at others, so compassionate. It was his serious attitude that baffled her so much at first. So very much like her father, and Trevor. Yet, with such a strong underlying sense of gentleness that she never quite knew how sincerely to take his words.

Or his touch. They shouldn't be doing this, holding hands. The smart thing for her to do right now would be to take her hand from his and leave.

But not yet. What a remarkable man, so full of life and promise of a great future. Beside him, she felt so unprepared to deal with her future. With his determination to succeed, his drive to do the best he could do, Burk intimidated her. She understood that, and knew that in some small way she was finally learning to stand on her own two feet. Coming here to Texas had been her first step. And she kept moving in the right direction. Breaking off her engagement to Trevor proved that. But could she ever stand up to Burk that way? She doubted it.

The best thing to do would be to keep her distance from him. Glancing down at their entwined fingers, she had to admit that she wasn't doing a very good job of that.

Burk led her west, away from the fountain down the center promenade. Ahead, a large bronze statue of a man riding a horse came into sight. The rider and horse seemed to be heading off into the sunset.

"You haven't answered my question," Burk said in the growing darkness as he brushed his thumb across the back of her hand.

"What? Your question?" Elizabeth's mind blanked. What could he be talking about?

"About your true feelings," he prompted her. Waiting for her response, he began to rub tiny circles on the back of her hand. "Are you still doing what you learned to do as a little girl? Are you hiding your true feelings?"

Alarm bells rang in her mind, and her face clouded with the unease his words caused. "I don't know what you mean, Burk."

"I'm asking if you're happy with your future, with your plans to marry Trevor."

"I—"

"Elizabeth, are you—" he bit off his words as another couple, strolling hand in hand, passed them. When they were far enough away to fade into the gathering darkness, and for Burk to feel comfortable, he continued, "Are you sure you should marry that guy? Do you love him?"

Swallowing hard, she tried to come up with some kind of answer to his probing questions. "I—I'm engaged to him, aren't I?" No, she wasn't, her conscience prodded her roughly. There was no love between her and Trevor, and they had no future together. But she couldn't tell Burk the truth. She couldn't risk putting herself in the vulnerable position of allowing Burk to know her true feeling for him; she had to convince him she still loved Trevor.

As that thought formed in her mind, Burk pulled her into his arms, and she went willingly.

"There's something I've wanted to tell you." He stopped, staring into the hazel depth of her eyes. "Elizabeth . . . " His hands rose up to tenderly cup her face, and he spoke his desire with his dark eyes.

Masterfully, his lips descended to her own, pausing a breath away. His touch, when it came, caressed so lightly, that at first she was unsure of what she felt. His lips, so ardent, and supple, molded themselves to hers. The warmth, the tingling warmth drew her to him, and she felt his hands leave her face to encircle her waist.

Hungry, then giving, Burk's kiss pivoted between tender and light, hard and demanding. Elizabeth wanted to feel him, to know him, to kiss him with all the desire that he ignited in her soul. But she felt the fear she recognized earlier that evening. It still echoed in her mind.

She couldn't let go, she couldn't return his kiss with the passion that burned inside her. Closing her lips to the tantalizing pressure of his tongue, she tugged herself from his embrace, and stood at arm's length from his tall figure. Burk groaned at his loss as his hands slipped from her back to a light touch on her arms, his eyes still closed.

"I think . . . I think we should be getting back. It's too dark to see any of the campus now." She felt like such a liar! Life, love, could be so unfair. This had to stop, or she might lose what little precious independence she had. Right now, she wasn't strong enough to have a relationship with Burk. It wouldn't be a casual relationship, not for her.

The one thing in the world she knew for certain now was the depth of her feelings for Burk. They were like nothing she ever felt before. Shattering in their intensity. At all costs, she had to keep them under control.

Heaving a painful sigh, Burk allowed his hands to slip from their tenuous connection with her arms. Raising his bowed head, his smoldering gaze found the shadowy outline of her face. "If you want to, then we will," he said, making sure she understood the decision to end their kiss belonged solely to her.

Awkwardly, she nodded her head, then realized it was too dark here in the twilight for him to see her. "Yes," she murmured softly.

"Then, let's go," he replied, almost achieving a light

tone. "Maybe I can bring you back here another time to see the statue," He took a step back the way they had come.

Glancing over her shoulder at the bronze silhouette, Elizabeth asked, "Who is the statue of?"

"It's Will Rogers." He stepped closer to her, but not close enough to touch, as he paused to look back. "He's one of my father's heroes."

"Will Rogers. He was a cowboy, wasn't he?"

"Yes, among other things," Burk answered. "He was a newspaper columnist in the nineteen-twenties, and an actor off and on. He even starred in the Ziegfeld Follies for a while." Burk smiled as he spoke.

Elizabeth circled the statue, gazing up at the open, friendly face, lit by the small floodlights in the ground. "He must have been quite a guy, to rate such admiration from people."

"Yes, he was," Burk agreed. "His most famous quote is, 'I never met a man I didn't like'."

"Really?" She turned from the statue to Burk. He stood so close, she could almost feel the warmth of his masculine body radiating through the night air.

"That's something I'd like to be able to say. But after meeting Trevor, I'm having a little difficulty with it."

His confession hung in the air between them, stunning Elizabeth with its simple directness. She shifted restlessly from foot to foot, trying to decide exactly what Burk meant by that. Did he dislike Trevor because of her engagement to him? Or was Burk's dislike of the man based on the fact that Trevor was, well . . . What was it about Trevor that she now found so disagreeable?

Trevor could be brisk, even rude. He was condescending, vain, and boorish. As she ticked off his traits, Elizabeth found herself wondering how she ever managed to tolerate a man like that for so long. But she never would again. Had it all hinged on her denying her true feelings? A great weight lifted off her heart when she canceled her engagement to Trevor. She actually felt lighter, she realized.

But somehow, she had to make sure she didn't fall into the same type of relationship ever again. Keeping her distance from Burk would be a very good start. Now, if she could just stick to her plan.

"Trevor can be a bit overbearing at times." She sensed that the safest way to handle Burk's comment about her ex-fiancé might be to pretend as if he could only have been talking about Trevor's personality. Resolutely, she chose to ignore the nagging, hopeful inner voice that wanted him to be jealous of Trevor. Jealous because of his engagement to Elizabeth, and the fact that he would marry her in December.

"I suppose," he muttered harshly.

His terse reply unnerved her. Would he let the subject drop now?

"We have an early morning tomorrow," he continued neutrally. "I suppose we should be getting back."

"Yes," she agreed, falling into step beside him as they made their way across the campus to the jeep. Surprisingly, Elizabeth felt little tension between them during the ride back. Maybe there was a chance for them to keep a good working relationship after all. Burk seemed willing to put aside what happened between them. Now if she could do the same. . . .

Chapter Nine

Burk slammed the book back down on the table by his bed. Ever since dinner last night . . . No, he wouldn't lie to himself. Ever since that kiss weeks ago, Elizabeth hadn't been off his mind for more than a minute. The frustration of wanting her was building to the boiling point in his chest.

Crossing his bedroom to the closet, Burk pulled a flannel Pendleton shirt from a hangar, and shrugged it on. The mirror on the closet door caught his reflection as he buttoned the green shirt, and he paused to assess himself. As usual, he wore brown work boots and faded jeans. His hair hung over his collar, too long, simply because he refused to take the time to have it cut. Brushing it back from his face, he noticed the dark circles under his eyes. Yes, he'd lost a lot of sleep since Elizabeth Way's arrival. It wasn't something he could blame on the demands of the job.

It was her. He felt the knot of frustration grow. Why?

Why hadn't she told him about her engagement? No ring encircled her slim finger. She hadn't sat around moping about missing her fiancé. Never once did she even mention Trevor, until that phone call. If he'd had some warning, he would have . . . he would have never allowed himself to fall in love with her?

Impossible. Nothing could have stopped it, short of sending her packing back to New York that first day. Even then, she would probably still be haunting his dreams. Turning his back on his reflection, Burk returned to the table and glared down at the book he'd set there moments before.

Damn! He picked up the offending book. A field guide to flint artifact analysis. He'd been trying to study it last night, and hadn't managed to absorb anything. His frustration spiked into anger and Burk hurled the book across the room. Its hard cover made a satisfying thud as it hit the wall. He picked up another book from the table and threw it at the same spot, uttering a curse as he did so. Then another book and another curse. He scooped up a discarded shirt from his bed and threw it at the door. Then a magazine, then a cup. The ceramic cup shattered against the wood and shards clattered to the bare floor just as the door flew open.

Ned stood in the opening, staring wide-eyed at the mess surrounding Burk. "Doing a bit of redecorating?" he asked.

"What's going on?" someone called down the hall.

"Nothing," Ned called back. "I just dropped something." With one foot, he scooted the ceramic debris aside and stepped into the room, shutting the door behind him. "I've seen you under stress from work before, buddy, but it's never gotten to you like this. Are you very far behind?''

"Far behind?" Burk snorted in disgust. "No. Things couldn't be better. In fact, the book is a bit ahead of schedule." He sank down onto the edge of his bed and continued buttoning his shirt.

"Then what's the problem?" Ned's brows pulled together in concern.

"Nothing," Burk answered belligerently.

"Then . . . Oh great!" Ned rolled his eyes in disdain. Stepping carefully through the pile of rubble that covered Burk's floor, Ned sat down on an antique ladder-back chair by the tiny window of the bedroom. "You've gone and gotten yourself involved with Elizabeth, haven't you?" The predawn indigo of the sky was visible through the thin curtains, and Ned sat back to study his friend. "I warned you about that, about the danger of getting involved with your assistant, but you obviously didn't listen."

"She's engaged," Burk snapped.

"Engaged?" Ned asked sharply. "If that's true, then how could something be developing between you two?"

"There's nothing between us, and there never will be anything between us. She's going to marry some jerk from New York when she's finished here."

"Some jerk? You sound as if you've met the guy. Have you?" he prompted when Burk remained silent.

"Yeah. He's a real weasel."

"Very scientific description, Dr. Sutherland. I didn't realize you were such a learned taxonomist."

Burk pulled his pillow from the bed's covers and threw it at Ned.

"Temper, temper," Ned chided his friend as he caught the pillow.

"I'm sorry," Burk murmured. "Honestly, Ned. I just got blind-sided by this whole thing. She's always on my mind. I can't seem to think of her as just an assistant and nothing more." His hands came up and his fingers wound in the dark tangle of his hair.

"Then you do have a problem, buddy," Ned solemnly said. "A serious problem."

Somehow, the work got done. Somehow, the next section that covered the Archaic Period, its cultures of people who inhabited the southern plains region and hunted with darts, got finished. Each page was typed perfectly. Each illustration was finished to Burk's exacting standards. Each photograph was labeled and placed in order.

They stood there, side by side in the office, staring down at the sealed box, ready to be mailed to the publisher. When it was gone, they would tackle the last two historical periods of Burk's book, the Ceramic and the Protohistoric periods. They were, by far, the shortest sections of the book, covering less than 2,000 years combined.

For the first time, Elizabeth wished the work weren't going so fast. The end of her time here seemed too real now, and she didn't want it to come.

"How about a celebration?" Burk asked softly.

A celebration? Like last time? Immediately, an image of them riding together on Nessy flashed into her mind. She could almost feel Burk's arms around her as she tried to stop the scene from playing like a slow-motion video. His hand came up to her face, and urged her to twist around in the saddle. His eyes shone down at her, their smoky depths hiding the flames she felt behind them. Burk's sensuous lips touched hers, and the image slowed to a stop.

"Shouldn't we get started on the Ceramic Period?" she asked, pulling her fingertips away from her lips. She squeezed her eyes shut, trying to erase the thought of that first kiss.

"We'll have time for that tomorrow." Burk moved around his desk to stand closer to her. "There's a cookout tonight in the compound. There'll be a bonfire, and hot dogs."

She could feel his breath on the back of her neck. "But that's not for a few more hours," she protested without turning to face him. "We could—"

"We could go to the farmer's market west of here. It's out by itself in the country. They sell a lot of local produce. We could get some watermelons for tonight."

Soft as velvet, his voice slid across her skin. She wanted to lean back into him, to feel the hard length of his frame against her again. Her hands ached to touch his broad shoulders, to touch the dark unruliness of his hair.

"It wouldn't take long. Come with me, Elizabeth," he compelled her, his voice barely above a whisper.

"Yes," she rasped out the word. I'll come with you. Wherever, whenever you ask, she wanted to shout. But she kept her thoughts to herself, and endured the painful pressure the unspoken words caused in her heart.

This time, he didn't take her hand, but she felt just as drawn along as if he had. The ride through the sparsely populated countryside wasn't long, Burk had said it wouldn't be. When they arrived at the market, he cheerfully instructed her in the fine art of picking out ripe watermelons, laughing at her attempt to thump the melon and listen for just the right resonating sound.

The smiles they exchanged came easy, with no hidden motives, or concerns in them. This might well be their last time to relax together, she knew, and she was determined to make it the best it could be.

"This one sounds good," Burk cheerfully announced as he loaded another melon in the jeep. "Do you think that'll be enough?"

"Don't ask me!" she declared. "You're the watermelon expert. I don't see how I've been of any help."

Laughing, Burk reached out and patted her on the head. "Feeling unappreciated? Don't worry, I'm aware of your hard work."

Elizabeth froze. He only meant it as a joke, she swore to herself. But the damage was done.

Burk saw the smile slide from her face, and his mood instantly sobered. Clearing his throat, he turned to go. "I'll pay for these, and be back in a minute."

As he walked away, she scrambled into the jeep, berating herself the whole time. Her reaction to his joke; that's what caused that look of pain on his face, and it shouldn't have. It had nothing to do with him. Burk never took her for granted. Trevor had exclusive claim to that action.

Burk drove along in silence, while Elizabeth searched for a way to get back that mood of easy camaraderie. "That's a mesquite tree growing by that pond, isn't it?" she asked, pointing out the window.

"Yes," he agreed. "You often see them around the playa lakes or some of the low-lying places in this region."

"Can we stop? I'd like to take a little piece of mesquite wood home as a souvenir."

"Sure, we've got plenty of time." He pulled off the highway and onto a narrow, dirt road that led in the direction of the small body of water.

They walked the last few yards over the rough terrain that surrounded the small blue pond. Elizabeth followed Burk through patches of tall prairie grass and around spiked, green yucca plants.

"How much do you want?" Burk asked, reaching up to break a thin branch off.

"Oh! Not that much," she protested. "Just a short twig, something that will fit—" Under her pillow, was what she had been about to say. Something she could keep with her, to remind her of the dinner they had shared, of burgers cooked over a mesquite fire. And the kiss in the dark.

"In your suitcase?"

"Y—yes."

"Will this be all right?" He held out a thin twig for her inspection. She stepped closer to take it from him. "Elizabeth—" he stopped, then lightened his tone. "Want to sit here for a few minutes?" he asked, indicating a fallen tree that lay near the water's edge.

"Sure," she agreed, trying to sound just as casual as he did. She joined him as he settled his long frame on the log. "It's beautiful out here, so wild and unsettled."

"It's hard to imagine what it must have been like for the settlers who first came to this region from back east, isn't it?"

Turning twinkling eyes on him, Elizabeth chuckled under her breath.

"What?" he prompted her.

"You." She smiled and laced her fingers over her knees. "I'd have expected you to be imagining a scene of First-view man butchering a bison out there somewhere."

"I'm not all work, you know." He arched his dark eyebrows comically at her.

Elizabeth started giggling, a silly school-girl giggle that usually embarrassed her so. Burk joined in and her giggle grew to a genuine laugh. He made her feel so happy. So satisfied.

"I want to tell you . . . " He leaned forward and rested his elbows on his knees. "I want to apologize for teasing you back at the farmer's market. I don't want you to think I don't appreciate you—"

"Trevor," she interrupted him almost too loudly. Then quieter, she began again, "Trevor was the one who never appreciated me. You have nothing to apologize for." She held her gaze steady on him, fighting the urge to look away from the keenness of his dark eyes.

His gaze fell away from her. "I see." Then his head whipped back up. "Was? Have things changed between the two of you?"

"Yes." Her heart rose up into her throat. "I've ended my relationship with him. We're no longer engaged."

Burk stared at her, open-mouthed. As she waited for him to speak, the silence that grew between them became deafening.

"You're not engaged any longer?" he asked, a bewildered tone strong in his voice.

Prodded by his question, Elizabeth managed to break the mesmerizing hold his eyes had on her. She stared at her hands, twisting together in knots of tension in her lap. Why had she admitted that? It was the last thing she wanted Burk to know. If she had kept her secret, she would have gone home soon, with him none the wiser.

But the pain in his eyes, pain she had caused by overreacting to his joke at the farmer's market . . . she couldn't allow that to last another second.

"Tell me, Elizabeth. You're really not engaged to Trevor?"

"I broke off the engagement when he was here."

"But, I saw you kiss him when he left," Burk argued, "he looked so happy."

"That was because I was assuring him that our canceled wedding plans wouldn't jeopardize any future business deals he might make with my father."

"And that made the clown happy?" Burk's voice rose to a thundering level. "He's worse than a weasel!" Slapping his palms on his thighs, Burk leaped up and paced back and forth in front of her. "He's a fool. He's an absolute fool."

Trevor wasn't the only one who fit that description, she reminded herself. She had been a willing partner in their miserable excuse for a relationship. She had accepted his proposal of marriage, and she should have known that it wasn't a relationship based on love. But rather one based on business and her inability to stand up for herself. She had been pliant to her parents' wishes, to Trevor's wishes, but no more.

Finally Elizabeth felt ready to stand on her own two feet, to try and be in charge of her own future. From now on, she would make her own decisions. But she still felt that core of fear deep inside her. Watching Burk storm back and forth on the narrow patch of clear ground in front of her brought that point out clearly for her to see.

Burk shared a trait with Trevor. They were both men used to going after what they wanted, and getting it. And when Elizabeth was part of that goal, Trevor hadn't hesitated to acquire her, like a piece of merchandise.

Maybe the fault hadn't been his. Certainly not completely. She had been there for the taking, just like something on a store shelf, she told herself. With no will or direction of her own, no life of her own. And she never wanted to be that way again.

With Burk, she feared she might lose the newfound resolve she had gained. He was so masterful, so self-assured. It would be so easy to let him take charge of their relationship, to let him decide what future they would have together, if any.

She knotted her tense fingers into fists. That was something she wouldn't risk. Now was the time to learn to take care of herself, before ever again allowing herself to be that vulnerable to a man.

"It's getting late, we should get back." She stood and began to weave her way through the brush back to the jeep. Burk's footsteps reverberated through the ground as he followed silently behind.

"There'll be music at the cook-out tonight." In the close quarters of the jeep, Burk's voice rang firm, determined. "Dance with me."

Was it a request, or a command? No. Burk never commanded. He didn't need to. What would it be like to be in his arms, out under the stars? The very idea intoxicated her.

"It's getting dark," she noted, saying anything to bring herself back down to earth. "Will we be there in time?"

"Sure. It's just over the next rise. Things should be getting started just about now."

And they were, she saw as she walked down the hill from the parking area to the compound. She held one of the green striped melons cradled in her arms as she walked beside Burk. They could see a large fire blazing merrily in the center of the clearing, and people milled about, visiting and unwinding after the full day they'd put in at the dig.

"Watermelon!" Clare squealed when she spotted Elizabeth and Burk approaching.

"There are more in the jeep," Burk said, thumbing over his shoulder.

"I'll get some help," Clare chimed as she affectionately patted the large melon in his arms, then whirled away to conscript volunteers.

"Let's set these on the picnic table," Burk directed Elizabeth. When their hands were empty, he tucked his arm loosely around her waist, and guided her to the ring of rustic, wooden benches that circled the fire.

"I've always enjoyed a campfire. Let's sit and talk awhile," he suggested.

Elizabeth sank down beside him, close enough for an intimate conversation, but not close enough for their bodies to touch.

"This morning Ned told me he would bring his CD player. He has a lot of country-and-western music." Burk placed his hands on his knees as he hunched his shoulders forward. His gaze flicked around the clearing, never resting long on one spot while he spoke. "I should have asked you . . . do you like to dance?"

The corners of Elizabeth's mouth lifted slightly before she answered him. "Yes, I do, if it's slow dancing. I've never been very good at the fast stuff."

"Good," he declared. "I mean, me too. So we should be just right for each other."

Just right for each other. The thought sent chills of anticipation up her spine. But that was followed swiftly by a sense of foreboding. It seemed clear now that Burk took the news of her broken engagement very seriously. Obviously he intended to deepen his relationship with her. But she couldn't allow that to happen.

"I really should go help with the cooking." Elizabeth glanced at the large grill and picnic table where a group of people were cooking hamburger patties and setting out bowls of chips. "It looks like Clare could use my help."

Burk leaned back to peer behind Elizabeth at the table. "Clare? I think she'd rather have help from one of those boys hovering at her elbows. Don't you agree?"

It was true, she acknowledged with a nod of her head. Clare had a certain way of attracting a large gathering of men, no matter what she was doing. As Elizabeth watched, two young men, probably college students, began helping her slice tomatoes for the burgers, and another who stood at her side tried to look needed by holding a platter for her.

Burk grinned at Elizabeth, and they both broke out in chuckles.

Finally, Elizabeth relaxed and leaned back. "I don't understand how she does it. I mean, I remember trying like crazy in school to attract even one guy, and failing miserably.''

"I find that hard to believe," Burk said as he shifted around to face her more fully.

"I mean it! I tried tons of makeup, French perfume, I even tried Kleenex. Nothing seemed to work."

"Kleenex?" Burk asked, wrinkling his brow.

Elizabeth flushed. "In my . . . '' She tugged the front of her blouse with her thumb and forefinger.

Burk's eyebrows rose in confusion. "Your . . . ? Oh!" he exclaimed. "Your . . . I see. Well, those boys must have all been fools."

She wanted to fan the heat away from her face, but folded her hands in her lap. "I was the one who ended up feeling like a fool," she admitted with a light tone. "I'm just glad I've finally grown out of that phase where all I could think about was the opposite sex."

Although, as far as the man sitting next to her was concerned, it seemed that she might be suffering a relapse. Apparently it started about the time of her arrival here in Texas.

Burk leaned closer. "I remember those awful phases too. I remember going to the senior prom alone," he confessed.

"You?" Now it was her turn to find his words hard to believe.

"Yep. I had this awful crush on this beautiful blonde. But she refused to acknowledge that I existed. Of course, it didn't help that she stood a full head taller than me." He smiled ruefully at Elizabeth.

"How tall was she?" Elizabeth asked, her eyes wide.

"Only about five foot nine. But I was only five and a half feet tall. I grew a bit in college."

"I'll say!" she exclaimed, staring admiringly up at the top of his head.

"There's Ned with the music," Burk said, pointing his friend out for Elizabeth, then he lightly draped his hand on her shoulder.

Trying to ignore the way her breath caught in her throat at his touch, Elizabeth turned to watch the archaeologist carrying a portable stereo and a stack of CDs. He set them on the table where Clare and her helpers were, and began selecting music with their help.

Moments later, the soft beckoning of an acoustical guitar rolled from the stereo's speakers, filling the compound. Without a second's hesitation, Ned pulled Clare away from the table and out into the clearing near the fire. Clare laughed in surrender as they began dancing to the slow music.

"Will you dance with me?" Burk asked as he rose and held his hand out to Elizabeth.

Out there, with everyone watching? She couldn't! But how could she resist? She glanced indecisively from Burk's towering form to Clare and Ned, comfortable in each other's arms.

Couples began streaming to the clearing now, joining Clare and Ned. It could almost be called a crowd, she realized. She and Burk would blend in with the others, be one of many couples holding each other close and swaying to the music.

Burk stood silently, his hand out to her, waiting for a reply. Never would she have imagined that it would be so hard to take a man's hand, but she knew she would do it. Leaning forward, Elizabeth placed her hand in his, her eyes lingering on the corded tendons of his masculine wrist. Effortlessly, he gathered her to his side, and brought her body to his. Slowly, they walked to the edge of the group of dancers.

With one arm wrapped behind her back, and the other cradling her hand, Burk encircled her. They danced. They moved together in lazy circles, twirling slowly, their steps in perfect symmetry.

Burk leaned his face down, closer to hers. "Are you enjoying yourself?" he whispered in her ear.

She felt the delicious contact of his warm breath brush over her sensitive lobe. "Yes, this is wonderful," she answered, her voice raspy.

"Good. So am I," he said as he slid his hand up her back and fingered the tips of her hair.

Elizabeth tilted her head back, feeling his fingers slide deeper into her chestnut tresses. His caress blazed a trail down through the thickness, stroking the back of her neck. Breathing seemed suddenly harder to do, as his touches sent new shafts of pleasure coursing through her.

It felt unbelievably sensuous, having Burk's hands on her, and at the same time almost scary to feel her arms around him. With an effort, she opened her eyes and gazed at his shoulder where her hand rested. She could see the firm set of his shoulders and feel the rippling of his muscles under her palm.

Slowly, she lowered her head to his chest, and spread her fingers, trying to feel more of him. She slid her hand closer to his neck, finding the throbbing pulse in the hollow of his throat. His heart raced as much as her own did, she realized.

Tearing her mind away from the sensations he caused in her body, Elizabeth tried to concentrate on his reactions. Now his breath felt almost ragged, and his muscles were like bands of steel. She felt the hard need growing in him.

"Hey, Elizabeth!" A voice startled her as someone tapped on her shoulder.

Jerking her head up from Burk's chest, Elizabeth saw Clare peering at her.

"I forgot to tell you. Your father called the main office here this afternoon. When the secretary couldn't find either you or Burk, she came to the dig and got me."

"Why?" Elizabeth asked, all too conscious of where she and Burk probably were when the call came.

" 'Cause your father insisted he be allowed to speak to someone who knew you personally. I fit the description, so I took the call." Clare smiled perkily.

"I'm sorry he took you away from your work," Elizabeth said earnestly, acutely conscious of Burk's arm still encircling her waist protectively. Behind Clare, Ned waited patiently for his dance partner to finish her chat.

"No problem," Clare assured her. "I'm glad I could answer his questions for you. It was really funny. He wanted to know how you were. Real specific questions. Then he told me to let you know he'd heard from your wedding coordinator, and that you should call home immediately. Sorry I didn't tell you sooner."

"Don't worry about it. I'll give him a call in the morning."

So, her parents knew the wedding plans were off. She

intended to call them, but felt unsure of the best way to inform them the wedding plans were canceled. She'd been postponing what she knew would be a very difficult conversation.

They would undoubtedly demand that she apologize to Trevor and beg him to go ahead with the wedding plans. That was something she would never do. However, telling them that she refused to follow their wishes would be so difficult for her. And she had just promised to call them in the morning.

She looked up at Burk, and saw that his eyes were locked on Ned. A strange emotion seemed to be glinting from his face. Turning to Ned, she saw a similar look reflected in his gaze. It almost seemed like a wariness, as if they were warning each other of some danger, and that rang bells of caution in Elizabeth's head.

Too soon. This feeling she had for Burk; she wasn't strong enough yet to handle it.

''Thanks for the message, Clare.'' Elizabeth gave her friend a light pat on the arm. Then she forced a smile on her face as Clare pulled Ned away, twirling into the crowd of couples dancing to the soft music.

The mood was shattered. A dryness filled her throat as she glanced up into Burk's smoke-colored eyes. He felt it too, the loss of the magical moment they were sharing. Now, the harsh reality of things irrevocably intruded, and drove it away.

Burk took her tenderly in his arms, and cradled her head against his chest. They danced, little more than a shuffle really, to the music, ignoring the sights and sounds around them. But Elizabeth knew that it was a vain attempt to recapture something that was gone.

They joined the others when someone announced that the food was ready. Elizabeth laughed and talked the rest of the evening, always aware of Burk's watchful gaze. She fought hard to talk herself into handling the situation, using her new sense of self-reliance she felt so proud of. It seemed to be working. By the time people began to clean up and go to their rooms, she had convinced herself that she would be able to handle the rest of her time here with Burk. She would be able to handle working closely with him, and even handle telling him good-bye when the time came.

Chapter Ten

" "D**o** you have that drawing of the bow and arrow hunters ready, Burk?"

"From the Ceramic Period?" Burk looked up from the pile of papers on his desk. "I can't find a thing under all this mess. We're going to have to take a day to clean up when we're through with this section."

Laughing at his look of dismay, Elizabeth joined Burk in his search. "I've got the pages that'll finish this section typed and ready, if you want to check them now."

"I'll do that after lunch." Placing the stack of papers he'd been searching through back on his desk, Burk rocked back in his chair and watched Elizabeth continue the search. "How about a picnic on the visitor's trail? I know a quiet, shady spot where we could go. We could take some sandwiches and colas down there. It'd be nice," he said, enticing her with a smile.

Since the day Elizabeth admitted to him that her en-

164

A Find for All Time

gagement was off, Burk had been persistent. He invited her to dinner, movies, and horseback rides. Twice, fresh flowers appeared on her typing table.

"If we get everything finished on the Ceramic Period, do you want to get to work on the Protohistoric Period this morning?" Elizabeth asked, ignoring his question.

"Yes. No, after lunch will be fine," he said, steering the conversation back in the direction he wanted it to go.

"All right." Elizabeth turned away and sorted through papers by her typewriter. "But I can't have lunch with you today. I have a few phone calls to make." She kept her back to Burk as she heard him sigh heavily.

"Another day, then?"

The disappointment in his voice was so clear that Elizabeth felt warmed and saddened by it at the same time. Burk wanted a relationship, and she didn't know what to do about it.

"There isn't much to do on the Protohistoric section, is there?" she asked, turning their talk back to work.

"Not much," he agreed. "I've gotten all the artwork done. The two photos of that section are tagged and in the box. It shouldn't take more than a couple of days to finish what we have left to do," he said with a note of finality.

They looked at each other in the silence that followed his words, each thinking of the different meaning those words held for them. For Burk, a beginning of a new facet of his career. For Elizabeth, the end of things here. Then, what? She didn't know.

"It's done," Elizabeth declared as she collapsed across her bed.

Clare looked up from the novel she was reading to see Elizabeth's melancholy face staring at the ceiling of the small room. "It?"

"His book. It's finished. He just put the last pages in the mail."

"Then why do you sound as if it's the end of the world?"

Elizabeth groaned. "I don't know. Yes, I do." She changed her tone as she sat up. "It's almost time for me to leave. Burk will get his directorship in Peru. He'll be going soon, and so will I. But in opposite directions," She protested, waving her hands in the air.

"Yes," her friend remarked, stretching the word out. "You'll be going back to New York and your fiancé. What's wrong with that?"

Elizabeth bolted up from the bed. "I'm not going back to Trevor!"

"What?" Clare asked, as she closed her book and slid to the edge of her bed.

"I've broken my engagement."

"I knew it!" Clare shouted in triumph as she leaped from her bed and clapped Elizabeth on the back. "You dumped that old stuffed-shirt! Good for you. Burk must be thrilled. I can't wait to tell Ned—"

"Tell Ned? What do you mean, 'Burk must be thrilled'?"

"Because he's in love with you, silly," Clare fairly trumpeted, hugging Elizabeth. "Oh, it's so romantic. Are you going with him to Peru?" She released Elizabeth and shook her head, adding, "Silly me. Of course you are. Has he suggested you meet his family first? You should have plenty of time to, before the two of you leave for Peru.''

''Slow down.'' Elizabeth firmly grasped Clare by the shoulders. ''You're wrong about Burk and me. There's nothing that serious going on between us. I broke up with Trevor because of Trevor, not because of Burk.''

''But . . . you do love Burk. I know you do,'' Clare cajoled her.

''I . . .''

''Elizabeth, why can't you say it? What are you afraid of?''

She sank down heavily on the edge of her bed. Clare dragged a chair over and sat down facing her. For a moment, they were silent, then Elizabeth looked at her friend. ''What am I afraid of? Of falling into the same pattern that I had with Trevor.''

''But Burk's not Trevor. That'll never happen. He's such a great guy.''

''I know he is, Clare. But I'm still me, don't you see?''

''No. I don't.'' Clare leaned forward, peering intently at Elizabeth.

''I'm afraid to get too close to him, to let him have the chance to take control of my life the way my parents and Trevor did. I don't feel strong enough to survive something like that again.''

''But you're one of the strongest people I know, Elizabeth. Do you really fear your parents' taking control of you?''

Elizabeth smiled slowly, then shook her head. ''No. Now that you've made me put it into words, I know that I don't have to worry about that any longer. I have control, and I won't lose it.''

''Tell me about it. Tell me why you're no longer worried.''

''I called off my engagement to Trevor while he was here.''

Clare sat up with a start, but managed to keep any new questions to herself.

''I know, I should have mentioned it to you. But I didn't want anyone finding out, especially Burk. Anyway, remember the cookout, when you told me my father had called? Well, he found out about the canceled engagement from the wedding coordinator in New York. When I called him back, he threatened to disinherit me if I didn't patch things up with Trevor.''

''No!'' Clare's eyes widened with shock.

''Yes,'' Elizabeth smirked when she answered. ''It was so typical of him.''

''What did you tell him?''

''I told him to marry Trevor himself, if it was that important to him. You should have heard him sputter. It was so hilarious, Clare.'' Elizabeth smiled, then felt laughter bubbling up inside her at her friend's expression.

Clare gaped at Elizabeth, then started laughing with her.

''Oh.'' Elizabeth wiped tears from her eyes. ''It felt so good. I told him I'd survive just fine without his money, and without Trevor.''

''I'm proud of you, Elizabeth. But it must have been hard.''

''Not as hard as I thought it would be. And in a funny way, I think my father respects me more for saying what I did. I've gotten a couple of phone calls from my parents since then, and they've been amazingly civil. They've never once pressed me to reconcile with Trevor.''

''That's great,'' Clare said admiringly. ''You stood up for yourself, and it all worked out in the end. So why don't you want to get involved with Burk?''

Elizabeth rose and paced restlessly to the window. ''I'm afraid. Not of him,'' she added, turning to face Clare. ''Of myself. How do I know that I won't allow Burk to take charge of things, of decisions I should make? Of my future?''

''You simply have to trust him, Elizabeth. And yourself.''

''I trust Burk. But, myself? I just don't know. . . . ''

''I got it,'' Burk quietly announced. He stood above her at the dig in the early morning hours two weeks later. Summer was almost over, and her time here as his assistant was days away from ending, too.

This morning, she came early to the dig to get a little excavating done before Burk showed up. Then he came, changing her whole world with his three little words.

''I got the directorship in Peru. The job's mine.''

Sitting back, Elizabeth gazed up into Burk's face, shielding her eyes against the morning sun that shone from behind him, giving his head a golden halo. ''You're going to Peru.''

''Yes.'' He knelt and looked at her eye to eye. Reaching out he took her hand that still held the trowel, pulling the tool from her lax fingers. ''Are you happy for me?''

"Of course I am," she hastily answered. "I know how much you've wanted this."

"And I know how much you've helped me to get it, Elizabeth." He spoke barely above a whisper now.

Nearby, other people were arriving at their units, preparing for a morning of excavating the layers of sediment that hid artifacts, clues to the lives of ancient people. Elizabeth became acutely aware of the workers, although Burk seemed to think they were completely alone here.

"It was my job." She stood, pulling her hand from his.

"It was more than that. I—"

"Let's take a walk," she interrupted him, scrambling to her feet and leading the way from the area of growing activity through the grove of elms surrounding the Lubbock Lake Site.

Burk followed close on her heels. "As hard as I drove you, Elizabeth, it had to be more than simply a job to you."

"What do you mean?" She avoided his gaze as she walked beside him, so very aware of his masculine gait. It seemed that he held back his ground-eating strides to stay close to her, but she could still feel his steps reverberating through the earth.

"I got so unreasonable when I fell behind schedule."

"No. That's not true," she chided him.

"It is, and you know it." He smiled down at her, but she didn't see. "I acted like a fool, a stubborn fool. I want you to know, without your help I would never have made it by the deadline. At least, not with something usable. And, Elizabeth, that book is superb. It's exactly what I envisioned it to be."

"It is great, isn't it?" she agreed. "I've never been a

part of something so important to me before, Burk. It gave
me a wonderful feeling.''

"And now? Now that the book's done, what feelings do
you have?''

Her breath caught in her throat. Was Burk asking about
her feelings for him?

"Elizabeth . . . '' He took her hand loosely in his as they
walked along in solitude. "How do you feel about us? I
want to know if you think we could have a future together.''

Oh! How she wanted that, a future with Burk. To have
him as a part of her life forever. The desire swelled in her
chest, threatening to overwhelm her. But he would be leaving soon, in a few weeks. For a while he would be in
Philadelphia, with his family. Then, he would be in Peru,
and she would be, where? She still hadn't decided.

"We could exchange letters. You could write me from
Peru. Let me know your address, and I'll send you mine.''
The words were so much less than she wanted to say.

"Write? I had hoped . . . '' Burk's voice trailed off.

"We should get back to work. I promised to help Clare
with some cataloguing this afternoon, and I don't want to
fall behind on the excavating.'' She stopped and looked
over her shoulder toward the dig.

Burk stood silently beside her, his gentle fingers tracing
a path from her hand up her arm to the side of her neck.
"Elizabeth,'' he breathed her name softly. "Do you remember that day at the playa lake? You told me you were
no longer engaged to Trevor.''

Her face clouded as she recalled the mixed emotions she
felt then.

"I realized you had waited all that time before telling me. I also realized you needed something from me. Time, you needed more time for yourself. I've given it to you, Elizabeth. And now it's time for us.''

Turning her desire-flushed face to his, she was struck by the brilliance of his storm-colored eyes. The morning light added to their foggy depth, and to the sense of leashed power Elizabeth caught a glimpse of every time he seemed tense, or uneasy. The tendons of his neck pulsed with the beat of her heart, creating a rhythm of tension she felt growing in the pit of her stomach.

She ached for him. She ached for the feel of his arms around her, the feel of his lips on her mouth. The sense of need became almost staggering, and Elizabeth locked her knees to keep them from trembling.

"Burk." His name rolled like a plea from her lips.

Silently, his mouth descended onto hers, his lips caressing her softness, heating the passion blazing up in her heart. Burk took her into his arms, crushing her to his unyielding chest, loving her more deeply than she ever thought possible.

Dizzying waves of wonder crashed against the surface of her mind. She was in his arms! In Burk's arms. And at last, he was kissing her.

Her hands roamed over the rippling muscles of his arms, winding their way up to his shoulders and the pulsing hollow of his neck that she remembered so well. Burk moaned under her touch, his mouth vibrating against hers. His firm lips searched hungrily across the velvet softness of her sweet mouth, caressing and exploring at the same time.

His response to her tender touch stunned Elizabeth. The

depth of the resonance she felt forming between her and this captivating man was so unexpected, so overwhelming. She felt almost like a small boat lost in a stormy sea. Such tenderness and such strong passion together, it was all so new, so unexpected. How incredible it all seemed, that Burk could cause the depths of feelings that were now stirring in her heart.

Timidly Elizabeth responded to his kiss, pressing her flushed lips to his. Higher she allowed her fingers to roam, up to the locks of his wildly tousled mane. The curling ends wisped around her slender hands, tickling her palms and wrists as she spread her fingers through the dark thickness.

Burk's broad hands encircled Elizabeth's slim shoulders. She felt his tremendous strength, restrained now as he gently traced lazy circles on her back. He held her like that, their lips pressed together, his arms brushing lightly across her skin. It felt so safe, so wonderful to be in his arms, to be kissing him. She felt herself relaxing, melting into his solid embrace.

Down through the thick, dark hair her fingers explored, feeling veins pulsing at his temples, then the slight raspiness of cheek bristles.

Full of the wonder of the precious moment they were sharing, Elizabeth broke their kiss, pulling back from his encompassing embrace, but left her hands cupped tenderly around his cheeks. Staring into his eyes, she felt her lips trembling, full and flushed from his kiss. This was a moment she would remember for all time, the first moment she felt she was beginning to understand what real love could be.

Was this what a man and a woman truly in love could feel for each other? A bonding so deep, so strong that nothing could ever come between them?

"Elizabeth." He formed her name as almost a question as he brushed a tear from her cheek.

She hadn't realized it had formed. Self-consciously, she brushed at her face with the back of her hand. "Allergies," she said, following the word with a broad smile.

He captured her hand and kissed the moisture from it. Then kissed her cheeks, first one, then the other. Pausing to gaze longingly into her eyes, he smiled, then kissed her lips lightly, reverently.

Leaning closer, he whispered in her ear, "Promise me something."

"Yes." Idly, she traced the veins on the back of his hands as he cupped her cheeks.

"Promise me that we can continue this conversation tonight."

"Yes," she repeated, with no trace of question in her tone.

A small crisis came up that afternoon. Ned dropped a bottle of ink on a stack of illustrations Burk had done for him. Immediately, Burk set to work recreating them from the preliminary sketches Ned kept on file in his office.

"I'm sorry to take you away from finishing up your paperwork," Ned said.

"Don't worry about it." Burk glanced up from his desk. "Elizabeth can take care of everything that's left for me to do before I leave here."

"Speaking of Elizabeth, where is she?"

"Helping Clare with some cataloging."

"Boy, there isn't much she can't do, is there?" Ned marveled.

Burk smiled and nodded in agreement.

"So?" Ned prodded his friend.

"What?" Burk glanced up.

"So, what about you two? The book's over with, and there's no reason not to get together now, is there? I mean, Clare mentioned Elizabeth isn't engaged any longer. Now the field is clear, so to speak."

"Things have been . . . developing." Burk finally found the right word as he managed to hold in a grin. "And it never really was a problem. As far as getting the book finished, I mean. Our personal relationship never got in the way of work. I couldn't have had a better assistant."

"You quit wishing for Jean-Paul to come back?" Ned teased his friend.

"Yes," Burk answered derisively. "Actually, she did the job flawlessly from day one."

"I've always been puzzled about that, Burk." Ned rose from his perch on the corner of Burk's desk and paced about the confining office. "How could she have come here, completely untrained and unqualified, and do the work that she's done? That just doesn't seem possible."

"I know." Burk put down his pencil and steepled his fingers together. "I had such an erroneous impression of her from her application. I thought she was much younger." He held up a finger for each point that he made. "I had the impression that she couldn't type. I also thought she had no education—"

"But she obviously had some experience in archaeology,

or paleontology,'' Ned interrupted him. ''Where did she get it? And why were you so wrong about her?''

Burk eyed the filing cabinet that held a copy of Elizabeth's application. He remembered intending to check it some time ago, but had forgotten about it. Pushing himself up from the desk, he stalked over to the cabinet and pulled open the drawer.

''Somewhere in here is a copy of her application, and the letter that came with it. I remember thinking that it was handwritten, but Elizabeth insisted it was typed. . . . ''

He pulled out a folder and returned to his desk. As he spread out the contents of the folder, Ned joined him, leaning over his shoulder to peer at the papers.

''Here,'' Burk exclaimed in triumph. ''Here's her application.''

''But it's handwritten!'' Ned declared.

''And look at this.'' Burk pointed at the paper. ''It says she's . . . nineteen!''

''No way,'' Ned scoffed. ''She's no teenager.''

Shaking his head, Burk continued. ''A finishing school in Europe, I know that's true. But no work experience, no college, no experience of any kind remotely related to archaeology.''

''Impossible, Burk. Somebody's playing a joke on you.''

''Or on Elizabeth,'' Burk reflected thoughtfully.

''But who?'' Ned asked. ''Who would do such a rotten thing?''

''I don't know, but I intend to find out.''

What Burk found out was that the subject wasn't easy to bring up. A week went by, and he still didn't know any more than he had the first day. During the days, Burk worked hard to finish Ned's illustrations, while Elizabeth worked alone at the dig. Their evenings together never seemed long enough to get out all the words they had to say to each other.

"Hi," Elizabeth called as she breezed in his office door late in the afternoon. "How's the work on the illustrations going?"

Burk looked up from his drafting table, drinking in the sight of her wind-tossed chestnut hair, and her long, tanned legs, perfectly exposed by her red shorts. "Just fine. I'm on the last one now."

"Good. Then you can finally get back to some real work at the dig," she teased him.

Smiling at her light mood, Burk rose, and helped her stack the sketchbook back on the high shelf by the door. "Have you missed me that much?"

Elizabeth's hazel eyes blazed as she turned to face him. "I have," she replied boldly. She bared her feelings to him, reveling in the sense of candor. It felt so good to speak her mind, to let him know how she felt about him with no sense of dread.

Smiling to herself, she shook her head. What had she dreaded about her feelings for so long? Rejection? No. The possibility that he would use her desire for him as a way to gain control over her? How foolish that seemed now.

Burk stepped closer, his hand seeking out her cheek, and drawing her eyes back to his. "I've missed you too, Elizabeth. And I've realized something. I suppose it's because I had to spend all these days away from you." He searched for the right words. Pulling his hand from its tenuous touch with her, Burk turned and paced away.

"I've realized that my goals have changed," he finally continued. "I don't want the same things I did when you first came here."

"What do you mean, Burk?" Elizabeth followed him, placing her hand on his shoulder.

He turned and gazed into her eyes again. "I need you to sit down," he said, backing away from her touch. "Over there." He indicated his desk chair.

Her mouth drawn down into a frown of puzzlement, and a little confused, Elizabeth stepped around him and sat down. Was he going to tell her he wanted to end their relationship now? He would be leaving in less than two weeks. But she had planned to spend the remaining time they had getting closer to him. She needed to build memories of Burk to sustain her while he lived in Peru. They talked more about exchanging letters, and she knew that would become very important to her. But, if he had changed his mind about her, if he wanted to end the precious thing that was growing between them . . . No, she couldn't even contemplate that.

"What is it, Burk?" Her voice quavered despite her efforts to remain calm.

"Before you came here, all I could think about was my work," he began as he paced back and forth in front of her, his hands raking through the sides of his unruly hair. "It drove me, consumed me. Every day and every night, all I thought about was my work. Then you came."

"And I changed all of that. I distracted you, got in the way." She stared straight ahead, her tone flat and lifeless.

"Oh, you distracted me," he agreed. "But you never got in the way." Abruptly, he stopped pacing and swooped down in front of her, turning the chair swiftly to face him. "Elizabeth, you've made my life so much richer, so much fuller." He stopped and rubbed a hand over his eyes. "I'm making a mess of this."

"I understand that you'll be leaving soon. It's all right, Burk—"

"No! It's not all right." He placed his hands on her knees. "You don't understand what I'm trying to say, because I'm making such a fool of myself."

She sat back, peering into his troubled face. Reaching a hand up, Elizabeth tried to wipe the furrow from his brow.

He captured her hand and kissed her fingertips, one at a time. "What I'm trying to tell you is, I don't want Peru any longer."

Her eyes flew open wide in shock. "No!" Had she somehow taken away his dream?

"Not without you, Elizabeth. It would be meaningless if I didn't have you by my side."

"By your side? You want me . . . ?"

"Yes, I want you, my love. I need you with me. I want you by my side always. I won't go without you. Please, Elizabeth, say you'll go with me. Say you'll be with me always."

"Oh, Burk." Elizabeth felt her bottom lip begin to tremble. She sucked it in between her teeth and held it there.

"If you can't bear the thought of leaving the country, then I'll stay with you." He took both of her hands in his and kissed her palms. "I'll find some work here—"

"No," she interrupted him. "That's not it. . . ."

"Then tell me what it is. What's making you reluctant to—" he stopped, rocking back on his heels. "I'm still bungling this. I hadn't meant to do this here in this stuffy old office. I meant to have you out under the stars at night. Or at some fancy restaurant, with champagne on hand."

"Champagne?"

Pressing a finger to her lips, he hushed her questions, then recaptured her hands. "Elizabeth, will you marry me? Will you be my wife?"

A pulse drummed in her ears. The room threatened to waver out of focus. Could this all be a dream? Burk clutched tighter at her hands. This was no dream. He was real, he'd asked her to marry him. Memories of her self-doubt skipped across her mind like stones across the surface of a pond. The memories were only reflections of something that didn't exist any more.

"Yes, Burk. I'll marry you," she whispered.

With a shout of joy, Burk caught her up in his arms and twirled her about the tiny office. He rained kisses over her face and neck, and finally sank into his chair, holding her in his lap.

"Dr. Sutherland, you can be a wild man, for such a stodgy old scientist. But I love it," she said, then kissed him on the nose.

"That's because I love you, Elizabeth."

"And I love you, Burk." She laid her head on his shoulder.

"Never stop telling me that," he said softly, his lips brushing against her hair. "I'll never tire of hearing it."

"I love you, Burk Sutherland."

He claimed her mouth then, with a kiss so deep it left her dizzy. Smiling at her flushed face, Burk brushed a strand of hair from her cheek. "I can't wait to call you my wife. I can't wait to introduce you as my wife to people we meet. It's such a thrilling idea.'' He kissed her lightly on the cheek where his finger had just been.

''Now there's only one question left. Do we get married here, or wait till we're in Peru? Hey, is your passport up to date? We need to make arrangements for joint housing there. Also, we should get you an application for a position at the dig. I'm sure there's something you can do there. There's always a need for volunteers—''

''Now wait a minute, Burk.'' She struggled to sit upright.

''But I thought you said Peru wasn't the problem. If you don't want to go, we won't,'' he reassured her as he reached for her shoulder.

Standing up, Elizabeth took a step away, wrapping her arms around herself. ''Leaving the country isn't a problem for me, Burk. It's just that, well, I've had enough of volunteer work.''

''But, Elizabeth, there may not be a position for you. You'd need a degree for most of the jobs down there, or at least more experience than you've gotten this summer. The funding is really controlled on a site like that. Wally—''

She wheeled around and planted her fists on her hips. ''Wally what? Do you think I couldn't get the job without Wally's help?''

''Elizabeth—''

''Oh my God,'' she interrupted him, her hand flying to her mouth. ''You do think that. And I know why.'' She turned and paced further away from him. ''Trevor did this. He caused this problem. If I hadn't known, if his meddling had caused us to break up,'' her voice caught in her throat as she looked back at Burk. ''Do you have my application? The copy you got in the mail?'' she demanded.

''Yes, it's in the filing cabinet,'' he answered as he went to the drawer he had so recently returned it to after looking at it with Ned. ''Here.'' He handed it to her.

''I should have straightened this out long ago.'' Her mouth tightened into a scowl as she studied the paper. ''I should have told you what Trevor did.''

''He switched your form. He filled out a new one, and put it in with Wally's letter. That's why this one's not typed, like you said it was,'' Burk guessed.

''Yes. When did you figure that out?''

''I suspected it a couple of weeks ago. But I didn't know what to do about it. What I can't figure out is, why? Why would anybody do that?''

''It was Trevor's warped way of trying to keep me under his thumb.''

''I can't imagine you under anyone's thumb, Elizabeth.'' He grinned at her when she shot him a surprised look. ''Now tell me the truth,'' he said as he took the paper from her. ''And make me feel like less of a cradle robber by starting with your age.''

''You already know that. I happen to remember the spectacular way I corrected that information right here in this office.''

Burk threw his head back and laughed with her at the memory of her fiery rebuke of him. His light-hearted words, that she would be bored by spending time with stodgy old archaeologists like he and Ned, had infuriated Elizabeth at the time.

''You're so cute when you're mad,'' he teased.

"I'll give you cute, mister!" she exclaimed. Her face split into a wide grin as she punched his rock-hard arm.

Burk retaliated by pulling her into an engulfing embrace, and kissing her breath away. "I like you breathless. I'll have to do this more often."

"You'll have plenty of chances in Peru. Especially since I intend to apply for the position of administrative assistant." Seeing the surprise on his face, she motioned for him to sit down. "I think I'd like to fill you in on what I've been doing since that silly finishing school in Europe."

Dusk settled outside as Elizabeth finished detailing her education and experience to Burk. At times, he grew angry at what Trevor had done to her, and interrupted her story with his rantings. But Elizabeth merely waited for him to calm himself enough to sit back down, and then she would continue.

"But my parents were so set against me doing anything useful with my life, that I felt the only recourse left open to me was volunteer work at the American Museum of Natural History. Actually, it couldn't have worked out any better. I got a wonderful grounding in so many aspects of archaeology and paleontology. I've worked with some of the top people in both fields. It turned out to be a fantastic beginning."

"Beginning to a career that you really want?" he observed.

"Absolutely," she agreed. "Now more than ever."

"And you'll make a terrific administrative assistant. I remember you mentioning that desire to me over dinner once. I was so surprised at your ambition then. But I know you better now, you're a person who makes things happen for herself.''

"Oh, Burk, you couldn't have given me a better compliment.''

"I mean every word of it. With the skills and experience that you have, you would be perfect for the job.''

"I think so, too,'' she agreed. "I relish the idea of being the person who keeps things going behind the scenes. I mean, being responsible for scheduling, equipment, supplies—it sounds like the most fulfilling job.''

"Elizabeth, you're a wonder.'' Burk grinned as he spoke.

"And I'll still have time to do a little excavating.'' She gazed through her lashes at him. "That is, if the director will let me.''

"Oh, I think he will. Somehow I think the director will be very understanding of what you want to do.''

"Really?'' She watched as Burk rose smoothly from his chair and came to her. He pulled her to her feet, wrapping her securely in his embrace.

"I think you and the director will get along perfectly, like husband and wife.''

"I love you, Burk.'' She sighed as his mouth descended to hers.

Just as the moist warmth of his lips touched her, he echoed her words, "I love you.''

"Wait,'' she said, pulling her mouth from his. "We haven't answered that one last question you had.''

"What?'' His eyes were clouded with desire.

"About when we should get married.''

"Tonight," he urged her, renewing his arduous caressing of her lips.

She shook her head. "On our way to Peru. I know a beautiful little chapel on the coast in Mexico. We could stop there on our way."

"Sounds marvelous," Burk murmured, then kissed her breathless once again.